By the s

Fı

The Mating Game
(with Jovanka Houska)

The Lost City of Cantia

The Ada Lovelace Project
(with Jovanka Houska)

Non-fiction

Jacquard's Web: how a hand-loom led to the birth of the information age

Spellbound: the improbable story of English spelling

Ada's Algorithm: how Lord Byron's daughter launched the digital age

(also published in Finnish, Polish and Spanish)

Writing Fiction: a user-friendly guide

Charles and Ada: the computer's most passionate partnership

Frankie: the woman who prevented a pharmceutical disaster
(with Sandra Koutzenko)

Libretto and lyrics

Ada's Algorithm: the Ada Lovelace musical

Rollercoaster

Rollercoaster

Published by The Conrad Press in the United Kingdom 2021

Tel: +44(0)1227 472 874
www.theconradpress.com
info@theconradpress.com

ISBN 978-1-913567-08-8

Typesetting and Cover Design by: Charlotte Mouncey, www.bookstyle.co.uk
The Conrad Press logo was designed by Maria Priestley.

Rollercoaster

a 1970s comedy thriller for the 21st century!

James Essinger

In affectionate memory of the brilliant
and inspiring literary agent David Bolt
(November 30 1927 - November 16 2012)

Many thanks, David, for all the encouragement
and help you gave me with my writing.
Rollercoaster was David's suggestion for the title of this book.

Also for Päivi Aho of Finland,
and for Elaine Varty, who back in 1979 enjoyed me reading to her the scenes featuring 'Pickly'.

My warm thanks to Francesca Garratt for checking the transcribed typescript of *Rollercoaster* for typos and verbal infelicities from 1979, 2019 and 2020.

Preface

You don't need to read very far into *Rollercoaster* to suspect that the author is (a) a virgin, (b) somewhat bonkers and the further you read into the novel the greater your conviction about (a) and the more inclined you are to think that in (b) the word 'somewhat' may be superfluous.

Reading the novel now, I don't really recognise the author at all. Which is something of a shock, as the author of *Rollercoaster* is, in fact, me.

Silja's parents' traumatic life stems from events in the winter of 1939, a few months more than forty years before I wrote the first draft of this book, in the summer of 1979. Another forty years passed before I re-read *Rollercoaster* and decided to revise the novel and get it ready for publication.

When I wrote the first draft I was twenty-one and living in a bungalow-type cottage in the village of Weston-on-the-Green, near Bicester in Oxfordshire, England. It was the summer holiday between my second and third year at Lincoln College, Oxford University, where I was studying English Language and Literature and consistently failing to find a girlfriend.

I'd moved into the cottage with some friends who weren't there most of the time, so I was quite lonely, although I did have other friends who came to visit. I'd fallen in love with an extremely beautiful lady student called Frankie the preceding summer term. Frankie wasn't interested in me, though I don't really blame her as I had no idea in those days how to woo women. I used to serve them Lapsang Souchong tea and would read D.H. Lawrence to them. It didn't work. It was only later in my life that I learned that the best way to woo women is to listen to them; well, assuming they want to talk to you in the first place.

I'd spent the previous two summers working for three months in West Germany: in the summer of 1977 with a restaurant and catering firm called Stockheim in Düsseldorf and in the second summer of 1978 at the Düsseldorf Hilton as a houseman, which meant I hoovered the rooms before the chambermaids cleaned them and did other jobs in and about the hotel, such as moving furniture.

Those two summer stays in West Germany made a massive impression on me. During my first summer there I met Finnish people, including a young woman called Päivi Aho. As I've grown older, I've come to believe they made me much more emotionally healthy than I was after my upbringing in the emotionally rather suffocating atmosphere of Leicester, in a household without any sisters and educated at a single-sex grammar school. My darling brother Rupert, who died in what was very likely a grotesque accident - while deeply upset about marital problems he drowned on 22 January 2019 in the Grand Union Canal in Leicestershire, about four miles from where he was visiting our mother in Leicester - never had the equivalent of my West Germany stays, and I think he could have benefited from a similar experience.

During my first stay in West Germany, I lived at a Stockheim-owned residence, sharing a room with one of my colleagues, William McCurry or 'Ginger' as we called him. He is still a good friend. That summer of 1977, when I was emptying some bins at the back of one of the Stockheim firm's outlets, I met a chap called Tim Connell from Keighley in Yorkshire - his German is and was great and at first I thought he was one - and we became close friends. Tim had much expertise with women and I learned a great deal of theory from him about how to get on with women, though it was some years before I could actually try to put this into practice. Tim wasn't working at the hotel during that second summer but he did visit Düsseldorf and we had some great times.

Rollercoaster wasn't the first novel I finished; I'd written one called *A Canterbury Tale* about two years earlier. I don't have that novel any more: I threw it away at some point. It was essentially an autobiographical novel based on the few months I lived in Canterbury in 1977 before going to university. I don't remember it as being very good or very interesting and I don't think the literary world is any the worse for its loss.

Rollercoaster was never put onto computer disk until I decided to publish it with The Conrad Press, the publishing firm I set up in December 2015 and which now has more than 160 writers. The daunting task of typing out my typescript of *Rollercoaster* was carried with characteristic efficiency by my good friend and colleague Margaret Dowley MBE. Margaret used to work for the police and so was used to pretty much anything. The original typescript, rather clumsily typed by me while I worked on it, was sitting in my various homes between 1979 and the spring of 2019, when I re-read it, intending to publish it if I thought it was worth publication and not if I didn't.

In many ways, after I wrote *Rollercoaster*, my literary career, such as it was, actually regressed for quite some time, partly, I suppose, because I actually went to live in Finland from 1980 to 1983. There, I spent a lot of time learning Finnish, a language I've deliberately kept up and am proud of being able to speak, though when I was living in Finland I did do quite a lot of writing - mostly short stories, as I recall - in my spare time.

As for being a virgin, I was fated to remain in that state until November 1982, when, in my second nine-month teaching stint in Finland, I went to live in the Central Finnish city of Jyväskylä. Despite having a name that sounds as if you've got a fishbone stuck in your throat - it is actually a wonderful university city. I lost my virginity there to a lady writer and editor. I was incredibly lucky; she was extremely passionate about me from the beginning. She was thirty-nine, I was twenty-four. I found our sexual relationship inconceivably exciting and vividly remember writing postcards to tell my friends in England afterwards how wonderful I thought sex was. For me, sex has never been something over-rated but was always remarkable and indeed continues to be so to the present day.

The short stories I wrote in Finland weren't very good and I don't have them any more. Basically, *pace* Dickens, Byron, Shelley etc, etc. I was a very late developer as a writer. I'm sixty-two now and still in the learning phase.

In the late 1980s and during the 1990s I made some of my living from writing non-fiction business books and management reports. I still wrote novels during that time but they weren't of a publishable standard. I don't think I ever re-read *Rollercoaster* at that point, although I never forgot it existed. I became a reasonably competent writer of non-fiction business books and management books and made a reasonable living focusing on those areas. I've been a professional freelance writer since 1988 and still am, though as I say I now run The Conrad Press too.

It was only in the early years of the twenty-first century that I finally wrote a reasonably successful non-fiction 'trade' book, by which I mean one suitable for the mass market. It is called *Jacquard's Web* and is the true story of how the Jacquard weaving-loom was central in inspiring the computer revolution. Since then I've written a fair number of narrative non-fiction works, including two books about Lord Byron's daughter, the computer pioneer Ada Lovelace, someone who greatly fascinates me. The first is *Ada's Algorithm* (2013), which has been optioned by Monumental Pictures for filming, and published in the US as well as the UK and also in Spanish, Polish and - coincidentally - Finnish. I've also published *Charles and Ada: the computer's most passionate partnership* (2019) about Ada and the nineteenth-century mathematician Charles Babbage, who designed the world's first computer. The second book contains lots of new findings.

One spring evening in 2006 I began writing a novel which after a ridiculous number of iterations and revisions was finally published in 2019, under the title of *Josh Moonford and the Lost City of Cantia*. By 2019 I had written two other novels I was reasonably proud of; one was a novel about a hero of the ancient world. I wrote it as a ghost writer so can't publicise the title here or the name of the person I wrote the book for, but it was published three times: twice in the UK and once in the US and sells reasonably well. I think one day it will get filmed as it's a very filmable story. That's because the story is extremely interesting rather than because my writing is particularly brilliant.

I also wrote a novel called *The Mating Game* between 2009

and 2016 which has been published in the UK and which has been sold to SB Entertainment in Hollywood. The screenwriter, Kevin Marshall, is currently working on the second draft of the screenplay. I wrote the novel but from the beginning the idea was that the authorial credit was going to be shared by my great friend Jovanka Houska, an international chess master, who in 2019 won the British Women's Chess Championship for the ninth time. The book is a first-person story about a beautiful young woman chess-player who at the start of the book has the problem that she only gets turned on by a guy if he can beat her at chess, which naturally rather restricts her socially.

The Mating Game is quite a merry romp and while there is some sadness in the book, it's generally I think a positive, life-enhancing story. Initially my idea was for Jovanka to have the sole authorship as a wedding present Jovanka married a Norwegian sex-god Arne Hagesaether in 2009. I was prepared to ghost-write the novel for Jovanka, but I spent so much time working on it over a long period, including two full one-year breaks from it while I was working on other projects, that I decided I didn't want it published without my name on it too, so we shared the credit although Jovanka's name comes first. I'm quite proud of *The Mating Game* and I think it was my first truly professional novel. I like writing as a woman; I'm not sure why.

I also wrote my next novel, *The Ada Lovelace Project,* as a woman, Lucy, who is from the year 2095 and who travels back in time to 1843. Lucy's epoch is dependent on an 1843 computer revolution initiated by Ada Lovelace actually taking place, and so Lucy comes back in time to try to make sure it does. I started writing what became *The Ada Lovelace Project* back in 2001, though the main story was different then; about a woman who had been a pirate queen rather the time-travelling Lucy, from 2095, anxious to make sure her world comes into being. I postponed work on the *The Ada Lovelace Project* to revise *Rollercoaster* and while I was planning on alternating work on both books, once I started revising *Rollercoaster* I decided not to stop until I'd finished the job. I like to have at least one book on the boil, so to speak, most of the time, though I do enjoy having breaks from working on a book too when. I can focus on more incidental types of writing and also on running my publishing firm, The Conrad Press, www.theconradpress.com

I finally finished *The Ada Lovelace Project* at the end of May 2020 and am also sharing the authorial credit for it with Jovanka.

I revised *Rollercoaster* rather than rewrote it - apart from the ending, which I did rewrite completely - though I did enhance other sections as I went along, and also cut quite a lot of material. But I didn't do a full rewrite, partly because I didn't think it necessary but also as I didn't want to give the impression that I was a better writer forty years ago than I actually was.

Of course, there are obvious improbabilities in the book, such as Tortoise hiring Terrapin in the first place and Erasmus Scales being able to speak Finnish. The latter huge improbability I'd actually forgotten about until I re-read the book.

There were various other places in the book where I forget the need to 'plant' a particular plot idea before benefiting from it story-wise. This is something I hadn't learned how to do back in 1979 and so I sometimes give the reader an implausible detail to absorb which I would have done better to have planted beforehand.

I won't say much more about *Rollercoaster,* except that some parts of it even now make me laugh, a great deal, possibly more than the passages from my most recent novel do. The cheerful squalor of the sexual relationship between Fox-Foetus and Vixen is I think quite entertaining, as is Vixen's bizarre physical appearance and the subsequent fates of both these characters.

As for Rod, I liked him when I was writing about him and I like him now: he's a cheerful, life-loving guy and I like Silja too.

After I wrote *Rollercoaster* I must have sent it to several literary agents. One of them, David Bolt of a literary agency that was then called Bolt and Watson, got back to me when I was back living humbly in Oxford, on Southmoor Road. The sojourn in the country had been all right for the autumn but when Michaelmas term (Oxford jargon for the autumn term) started, I found I needed to live in Oxford again in order to do my university work.

David wrote me a wonderful letter about the book, offering to take it on for representation. Unfortunately I seem to have lost the letter, although I've tried hard to find it since working on *Rollercoaster* again but have been unable to do so. I remember with great vividness the utter delight with which I read his letter. Among other things David said the book was 'very inventive' especially as I was 'still at college'. I originally called the novel *The Nose on Legs* which is not really a very good title for the book though OK for a chapter. It was in fact David who suggested I call the book *Rollercoaster*. As he wrote cogently and accurately in his letter to me, 'The book's not really about Fox-Foetus, is it?'

David did take *Rollercoaster* on for representation, though he didn't manage to sell it. That was lucky, really, as it gave me the opportunity to re-do the novel forty years later.

David was a highly successful agent. He was, for example, the agent of the famous bestselling writer, the late Colin Wilson. David was also a writer of fiction and non-fiction himself. His *Authors' Handbook* (1986) is excellent; a revised edition, the *New Authors' Handbook,* containing much updated material, was published in 2001.

David had an interesting and varied career before becoming a literary agent. He was educated at Dulwich College, served with the 10th Gurkha Rifles and was a superintendent in the police of Malaya (now Malaysia) from 1948-50. I met him, as I remember, at least twice, once at the Savage Club in London (I may have met him on another occasion there, but I can't quite remember) and once at his lovely home in Surrey. I never knew David especially well, but I feel very privileged to have known him at all.

David died in 2012. I dedicate this edited version of *Rollercoaster* to him, with great thanks, for encouraging me with my writing at a crucial time of my life.

I shall always be extremely grateful to David, who encouraged me to think and hope that maybe I could write stories which people would find interesting and enjoyable to read. I still continue to think and hope this every day.

James Essinger   January 2021

Rollercoaster

1

The white-haired man

Late June, 1979. Marseilles. Early on a Friday morning. Already a thick haze of sun, dust and sweat swirling up, climbing above the Canabière. Noise and haste along the streets; cars leaping and jumping in starts to the traffic signs. Over everything, the sun, still lying behind cluttered roofs, ready to sweep into the deepening blue sky. On the left of the great city artery, a shanty town of Africans - men and women, boys and girls on the make - shoe-shiners, cripples, cured but maimed lepers and children running for a bite of bread and a bowl of coffee. On the right, the native French side, weary shopkeepers unrolling window blinds, motorbikes slaloming around lorries, vans and cars. Crates slung in the road, fruit baskets flicking rotting tomatoes.

More dust. The sun rising still. Another summer morning. Far out to sea the rich of the bay breakfast on cereals, chocolate and coffee aboard yachts that sway like slow-motion galleons, guided by the latest navigational equipment, shipped direct from America by one of the hundreds of little firms that scavenge for trade by the walls and seashells of the docks and ports.

In the midst of such life, a man walked quickly towards a tiny baker's shop. He had made the journey often. He was buying rolls and butter for the first meal of the day. He might have been French, but his white hair, white skin, and white beard suggested something else. Arriving at the shop, he picked up a small package from the counter, and put a few coins in the package's place.

The white-haired man was a regular customer.

Not bothering to check inside the package, he turned from the counter towards the door. All in a quick motion. It was a promising to be a hot day and there was much to do.

'*Monsieur*.'

He stopped, turned round to the counter. The woman there, fat and old as the great ovens at the back of the shop, averted her eyes from his face, in a hurry.

'Yes?' The white-haired man was annoyed now.

'*Monsieur*,' again, but she did not look at him. 'The telephone.'

'For me? Now?'

'*Oui, monsieur*.' There was a guilty tone in her voice. An old customer, and being disturbed with jokes of this kind on a day when there was so much to do.

'There must be a mistake. You are perfectly aware I have no calls expected here.'

'*Monsieur*, the telephone.' Repeated.

The door was two metres away. Best thing to simply walk out furiously, and vow never to buy bread from that place again. There were many shops in the quarter that sold the few rolls and croissants he needed each day. That and coffee. But a telephone, ringing for him. Perhaps news, news from the past. Perhaps.

'Very well.' The man laid his package on the counter, and marched to the tiny office. Thirty seconds would be enough to deal with this ridiculous situation. A telephone call at his baker's shop! Indeed! And so early on such a hot day!

He picked up the receiver. The woman was in the same room, squashed against the door. But now her eyes were firmly turned on his face.

'There is no sound!' he snapped. 'I am busy!'

Busy. Too busy to hear a rush of gas from inside the receiver quieter than a bee's whisper.

His hand stiffened on the receiver, his mouth fell open. As slowly as a coffin moving to the incinerator, a trickle of red dripped from the side of his lips. He coughed a few times, clutched both hands to his throat and let out a choking yelp as a torrent of blood swept from his mouth. No time for words. He fell, missing the side of the counter with his head by an inch.

As he lay there, blood slowly streamed frothy clots of crimson from his face. And only then did the woman turn her eyes away. How ugly he was! Now that the fascination of his death was over, she saw only the ugliness. The ugliness; why in all the years he had bought bread from her the woman had never, quite, had courage enough to look at him full on, not early in the morning.

In five minutes, with the help of her obese son, the floor was cleaned and the late white-haired man was removed.

The woman was merely an agent, an utter minion, who knew nothing of how he had been killed or why. Her fee was only provided on the understanding with her contractor that any mention of the incident to anyone but her son would result in the permanent extinction of her bread shop, her and him.

The victim was a Finnish man called Vilta, and if he had ever had a surname it had long been forgotten. Such a thing belonged to his past, and in life he had not liked voices from the past. The present was enough to cope with. The past held a surname, another land, other people.

And the face.

2

Past not taken into consideration

It was later the same day now: a bright June Friday afternoon, in Canterbury, Kent, south-east England. Children ran and played, cameras snapped and great gulps of milkshake swilled down throats, but Charles hobbled along the road, penniless. It had been a bad few months. Charles's financial resources, always verging on the negligible, had reached the point of absolute zero. The most valuable thing he had about him was half a melting icecream, which he had snatched from an unsuspecting innocent toddler a few minutes ago while its mother's back was turned and which a Kentish sun was rapidly turning into a sticky multi-coloured slosh, dripping red and yellow from Charles's mouth.

Canterbury in the full swing of the summer of 1979 was a good place to be. If you had money. If you had friends. Neither of which Charles had.

'Not even enough for a beer,' he muttered in confirmation to himself. He had turned his pockets out long ago, and perhaps in the cotton there were still molecular cupro-nickely traces of the time when Charles's pockets contained money. Vanished memories.

Charles was on his usual afternoon futile walk around the centre of Canterbury. He watched the gutters, hoping to find something spendable in them, hoping to find something. Most gutters are full of bird droppings and decayed leaves, and though Canterbury be ever so saintly, the gutters there contain much the same. Teetering, and swaying like a field of rotten parsnips in a hurricane, Charles manoeuvred along Sun Street, and down towards Canterbury Cathedral. And as he swayed, the cathedral, symbol of everlasting faith, hope and French stone, remained placidly sublime in its foundations. A guardian of peace, and of sobriety.

Charles, failed grocer, failed housebreaker, failed husband, general failure, had come to Canterbury because he may as well have come to Canterbury. It wasn't too far from Margate, where he had spent the previous night on a beach and it wasn't too far from Gravesend, which would be his next one. Canterbury would do as well as anywhere else, its bushes were no less comfortable than anywhere else, and being penniless was about equally as bad wherever you chose to spend your day.

There was a half-full glass of beer on a nearby outside pub table, evidently neglected. Charles walked by it, looking as bland and unconcerned as any man in a dirty grey raincoat and threadbare shoes can look. Then he doubled back towards the table. The beer was five feet away. Three feet, and he prepared for the casual grab. Got it. He swigged it down in one slurp. It was stale, warm, and the rim of the glass was covered in some smeary substance that was rather unsavoury. But at least it was alcoholic. Charles felt a little better after sinking it down. He glanced round at the group of tables in search of another one. There was nothing, only a small tribe of boys.

'Enjoy yer beer mister? Who giv it yer then, eh?'

'He won't answer, he's a dafty!'

'Dafty! Bloody tramp more like!'

Tramp! The word smote Charles on the forehead and rammed through his body in a spasm. Tramp! He, a tramp! The urchins had run away, but the word was left in the air like a bad smell. Anything but that. Now, 'tramp' was written on all the nearby shop signs, and on the smiles of even the prettiest women walking towards the cathedral. In a sort of half-drunken despair, Charles wandered onto a wooden bench (on which a dove had just relieved itself), sat down and leaned to his left, onto the arm-rest.

No illusions now. This was rock-bottom. No more cheating himself with what might happen, or pretending that the past had not been so bad after all.

The past, Charles's past was simply a succession of failures. After a partnership with Alfie Bent in Scrumptious Groceries in Luton had failed, after a brief period as a robber had ended in disaster (Charles having believed the guard dog to be a stuffed ornament), after the liaison with Miss Betty Stiggs had collapsed (Charles having married 'her' and discovered on their honeymoon that she wasn't), now, there was nothing left. Amidst laughter, fun, gambolling couples, Charles was sitting futilely on a bench.

Having no future at risk, and no past to sacrifice, a post-card with scrawled copper-plate handwriting on it, in a shop window close by, caught his attention at once. He got up, went to the window and studied the postcard as intently as a condemned man searching for the date of his own hanging. Charles noted the message, the name, the address, everything.

WANTED. RELIABLE MAN.

PAST NOT TAKEN INTO CONSIDERATION

Apply to Dr Tortoise
13 Cathedral Walk

It would do. The chance of something, at last. Charles returned to his bench, wiped away some of the moisture he had left behind him and politely asked a shopkeeper in a nearby antiques shop where Cathedral Walk was. The shopkeeper, anxious to get rid of him, told Charles quickly and clearly, anxious to minimise the danger of him coming back.

3

Rod

The same June Friday. Late evening. Hammersmith, London.

Becky was panting like crazy. 'Got any more olives?' she managed to blurt out.

Rod was cool. 'Two, just two left.'

'Gimme,' said Becky.

Rod put two more olives into her red, sucking mouth. 'What a good sloz you are!' he yelled, pushing the olives right in.

'Sloz?'

'The best bit of sloz this side of Kensington, yeah.' Rod had tossed the olive bottle away and was now moving in for the attack once more.

Sweat poured off them both as Rod threw the duvet onto the floor, twisted himself around, lifted Becky up and politely went in. Quack, quack, quack, like two ducks flap-flapping across a wind-swept lake, they dripped water and flew into the realms of loin-filled torsion, deep, utmost ecstasy, and sex.

Rod exploded first, slamming Becky's head up and down on the duvet in his eagerness. A morsel of olive juice ran down her lip and onto the smooth linen beneath. Exhausted, Rod lay on top, looking at a picture of Millais' *Ophelia*, a poster, on the opposite wall.

'Again,' said Becky, slowly. 'Just once more.'

She opened her eyes, shut them again. 'I don't need any more olives.'

There was a love-bemused gleam in her eye and a half-smile on her face.

'Again, dab?'

'Please.'

'Dab, I can't again. Not yet.'

The girl glanced at Rod's mass of hair sprawled over her breasts and neck. How romantic he was!

Rod rolled off the duvet onto a Lebanese goatskin rug on the floor. The rug hadn't been properly cured and smelt most peculiar.

Becky said, 'when I'm with you, Rod, I think of far-off places, like Majorca.'

Rod said, 'Great. Great, dab, I reckon I'd yawn the mud for two nights to get my splicer in a squeeze like yours.'

Becky had not the faintest idea what he was talking about, but she assumed it was a romantic speech and anyway she was completely naked, except for her contact lenses.

On the bed (Becky) and on the floor (Rod), they both rested for some time, emitting little kitten-like murmurs of happiness. By Rod's head were five olive containers, the price he had paid to navigate Becky's virginity.

'When I'm with you,' declared Becky, 'time doesn't matter.'

Rod looked at his watch. It was ten past eleven in the evening and the next one was coming at quarter past. He stood up, hopefully, but it was really impossible to have Becky again. Sometimes, he reflected, you can just ask too much of your splicer. Not without a touch of regret. There was something particularly cream about having a virgin, to boldly go where no man had gone before. But it was no use. Rosemary, for whom Rod did in fact have the odd stirring of affection occasionally, was arriving in five minutes.

Becky's eyes ran wistfully about the ceiling.

'Such a nice ceiling!' she said. 'So white, so white and pure.' Choked with feelings, she said, 'How I love you, Rod.'

Twenty seconds later, Becky was clutching her handbag and stumbling down the stairs. Five olive bottles fell down the steps behind her.

Rosemary had brought a curvaceous female friend in a crimson dress. The friend didn't introduce herself. Rosemary was wearing only a black lace dress and a curious, animal-like perfume that reminded Rod of hitching in the early morning past Battersea Dog's Home.

'You look tired,' said Rosemary. 'Been busy?'

'Working.' Rod let them both in. His flat had two rooms, the bedroom, and the kitchen, which had a lavatory and a sink perched between the cooker and refrigerator. Rosemary and her friend waited in the kitchen, leaving their few outdoor garments by the sink while Rod gave them both a strong shot of a blue liquid he kept in a milk bottle.

'Is this any good?' Rosemary asked.

'You'll find out soon enough, dab, soon enough.'

They all went to the bedroom and sat down on Rod's bed, so recently the scene of a young girl's first deeply moving sensual experience. Rod had put a pillow in the middle, to cover things up.

It was the time of conversation. A visit to Rod's always ended in much the same way. It was only this initial period that was a little difficult and embarrassing. Rod was wearing the things he wore all the time – a waistcoat of camel skin, and dirty jeans. Outdoors, he wore a denim jacket too. He also wore a necklace threaded with beads of dubious origin, and a piece of off-white elastic that made his long, straight light brown hair into a ponytail. Rosemary and her friend sat on the longer edge of the bed, swinging their legs in harmony, hands pushed in close between their knees.

'Working?' Rosemary asked, while Rod fiddled with his beads.

'On my rucksack. A pocket needs mending.'

'You going off again, then?'

'Maybe. Maybe not.'

Rosemary's friend, still refusing to introduce herself, looked at a poster on the wall behind. 'Who painted that?' she asked, pointing at it.

'Millais, Victorian guy,' said Rod. 'Want some more stuff?'

'Please,' said Rosemary's friend, giggling.

'What's wrong, Sue?' Rosemary asked her (so that was her name).

'All those flowers!' she cried.

Rod and Rosemary glanced very quickly at each other. Rod tried to indicate *EXACTLY WHO IS THIS?* in one-tenth of a second, while Rosemary attempted to convey, *IT'S ALL RIGHT. I KNOW SHE'S STUPID BUT SHE'S CUTE, ISN'T SHE?* without Sue noticing. They didn't. 'What you looking at each other for?' demanded Sue.

Rod stood up and poured out some more of the blue liquid.

'Clean the sink with it, do you?' Sue asked.

Rod and Rosemary ignored her and she slowly finished the milk bottle, sitting on the bed and smiling now and then.

'Why you going off, then?' said Rosemary.

'Cramped, need to travel, get out.'

'Bored?'

Rod thought for a moment. 'Only in the mornings.'

Rosemary tried the nearest she could get to a concerned expression. 'The mornings?'

'Yeah, when the light's bright. Then I start thinking.'

Rosemary was tired of this. Although Sue was not yet fully drunk, Rosemary went and sat on Rod's knee. 'Better now?' she asked.

'Yeah,' said Rod, which wasn't true. 'Thanks, dab. Cream.'

Rosemary gently bit the back of his neck. 'Coaster,' she said, 'when will you ever stop using those ridiculous words?'

'I like them,' Rod replied, but the fact that Rosemary had used his surname (a sign of the deepest intimacy) meant that the conversational part of the evening was over. Without getting up from the chair he altered two electric switches behind him and the room was bathed in a sharp, slightly creepy orange light.

'Good,' was all Rosemary said, and she set to biting the back of his neck again, less gently.

Rod put his arms around her and hugged her. Sue, with the empty milk bottle on her lap, watched them, fascinated. She sat there during the next ten minutes, her mouth open like the proposed Channel Tunnel, then dived in.

Rod couldn't see her, as Rosemary's belly button was at this point positioned just over his eyes, and the first thing he knew of her appearance was a vigorous pulling sound somewhere below. He looked along Rosemary's side; Sue was holding his jeans. Now she hastily started tugging his pants down. He didn't have time to yell anything because Rosemary, in a quick movement, doing something she'd never tried before, pinched his nose with both her hands and stuck her tongue somewhere down his throat. Rod surfaced for air, blue and coughing, by which time Sue had come from underneath Rosemary and ripped off what was left of his clothes.

It was still dark, sometime around three in the morning, when Rod woke up. Through the window, he could see the London night, television aerials and window frames shot through with moonlight. For quite a long time he lay, breathing quietly in time to the heavy contractions of the two women. Then Rod wondered why he couldn't move his arms. He was somewhat surprised to find the dressing-gown cord still there, but the knots had worked loose during Sue's final collapse onto him. After a little pulling away he was free.

Free.

Rod had one especially vivid image of freedom. He thought of a Mexican bead-seller he had once seen in the Portobello Road. The man did almost no business, charging far too much for very bad stuff, but he made a fine living from tourists taking photos of him. Rod had gone down Portobello Road every Sunday for several weeks. He met most of his slozes there but it was the bead-seller he really went to see. They became sort of casual friends. One Sunday the man had gone, vanished like a train, and Rod had stood by the space where the man had been. Nothing was there but a few crisp packets.

How cream it would be to be free as that bead-seller!

Theoretically. But as Rod prised himself away from Sue's warm sleepiness, he reflected that there was also a great deal to be said for having a bed of your own and a sloz, or in this case two. The thought lasted a few seconds. Alongside Sue and Rosemary Rod saw June, and all the others who had ended their evening, or afternoon, panting and asleep on that bed. Nice girls, some of them, quite a few of them virgins, who had looked to him to show them, in real form, what they had spent most of their time from the age of ten imagining, or so Rod himself imagined, anyway.

Rod splashed cold water on his face. Increasingly nowadays, the image of the Mexican bead-seller came back to him as a strange, mysterious, inspirational figure.

But exactly what the Mexican bead-seller meant, Rod didn't know.

Taking care not to wake the two women, Rod looked for some clothes. His outfit was exactly duplicated in the drawer, apart from the pants. He had several pairs of those.

He quickly finished sewing the hole in one of the pockets, then he packed the now mended rucksack. Everything he needed he put into his luggage: passport, a few clothes, and beads.

Rod looked round the room once more. The rent was only paid until the end of the following week. He was better out, and he knew there was nothing much to say goodbye to. On the point of going, Rod went back and found a bit of paper and a biro. There was nothing much to say either, but he left a brief message for Rosemary and Sue: *I'm off. Don't know where. Ta for the slozes. Rod.*

Outside, it was very dark behind the street lamps. A few cars rattled lazily to work. As Rod walked quickly to the main hitching road, he had an idea that he had done all this in a dream, a long time ago.

He arrived at Dover by late morning, had some fish and chips from a chippy near the Western Docks, then prepared for the long wait until it was dark, when he could hitch a ride from a lorry that would be crossing on the ferry without a customs throb spotting. He wondered whether the Channel Tunnel would ever get built.

He spent much of the afternoon sleeping, his rucksack as a pillow, behind a large hoarding advertising Sealink ferries.

Night finally came. Back at the docks, the articulated lorries were lining up in a massive oil-reeking queue, slowly being gorged by the ferry's massive open rear. In the cabs, sleepy drivers occasionally peeped out from curtains. Engines revved, a few radios chirped out a background of pop music, and Rod stuck out his thumb, seeing the hand of the bead-seller that beckoned from inside the cab of every lorry that passed him.

The lift finally came from a sniffing Bulgarian man called (he said) Vassil, who talked incessantly to Rod in English so bad Rod couldn't understand more than about one word in twenty, as the lorry waited in the queue to board the ferry. Vassil spent most of the two-hour journey to Calais trying to find Rod on the ferry, and Rod spent an equal amount of time trying to avoid him, for according to a fundamental law of cross-Channel hitch-hiking, Rod, though a perfectly warm-hearted person, had naturally ignored his lift-provider once he, Rod, was on the ferry. Eventually Vassil, who never got any hitch-hiker to listen to him more than Rod had, drowned his sorrows in a cup of Sealink tea.

The ferry travelled on into the night. It docked at about two o'clock in the morning. Once Rod had escaped from Vassil, Rod spent the rest of the night asleep under a bush on the outskirts of Calais.

The first thing he thought when he woke up was how nice it would have been if there had been a dab beside him. But the bead-seller was calling.

4

Dr Tortoise

'About the advert in the shop window. The postcard.'

'Ah, yes. Come in.'

At about three-o'clock on the previous Friday afternoon in Canterbury, the door to 13 Cathedral Walk had creaked rustily open and Charles found himself in a tiny entrance hall that smelt very musty. His host, having allowed Charles only the briefest glance at him, at once disappeared into a side-room on the left, and Charles followed. The musty smell was stronger here, but much more curious was the room's decoration. The walls and ceilings were covered in hundreds of small photographs. They were all of the same young man, who was smartly dressed and smiling, against a background of bright sky. A mass of identical eyes stared at Charles.

'When did you see the postcard?' Dr Tortoise asked.

'Just now.'

'And you came here immediately?'

'Yes.'

Charles's host now sat down by an ancient wooden table, leaving Charles standing. He peered at Charles for a moment, and then said:

'Why?'

This sounded like an important question. Charles paused.

Past not taken into consideration flashed through his mind. It was a good chance. No point rushing things.

'Why?' repeated his host, turning his glare from Charles and looking around the room, slowly, at all the tiny portraits on the walls. It was the first chance Charles had to have a good look at the man who had opened the door. There was only a weak electric light overhead. The man had a grey pallor over his face. His eyes were almost shut. He had a thin, wizened face and large, long ears, which were like those of a gnome. Yet what arrested Charles's attention most of all were his limbs. Shrunk, screwed up and thin as sticks, his arms reached right over the desk. When he sank back in the chair, the string-like fingers trembled up and down on the blotting paper. When the old man spoke, his words seemed to issue from his chin, so small was his mouth. Only his fingers, constantly on the move, had any serious life in them.

'Why?' the man asked again. 'Why were you in such haste to come here?'

'May I have a drink?' Charles asked, trying delaying tactics.

'In a moment. You may also sit down, when you have answered my question.'

No choice now. 'Because of what it said,' Charles said truthfully. '*Past not taken into consideration.*'

'And is that you?' asked the old man.

'Yes,' said Charles.

The old man was silent. A few moments later his fingers picked up something from the table and he stared sadly at it. He put it down. From where he was standing Charles could see that it was a portrait of the same young man, blown up to a framed size. The man then pulled out a tray from behind the desk and poured Charles a double whisky.

The glass was dusty but not smeared. Charles preferred gin but he splashed the drink down immediately. Then he sat down on a chair behind him.

'My name, as you will have surmised, is Tortoise,' the old man said abruptly. Charles did not actually know what 'surmise' meant. 'Dr Tortoise,' the old man added. 'I have had that postcard in the window for some time, for some months in fact, but you are only the second person to answer it.'

Charles decided not to ask Dr Tortoise who the first person had been, and what had happened when Tortoise met him. So Charles said nothing. He was thinking that the old man looked more like a spider than a tortoise.

'I imagine people are suspicious of a job that requires no past experience,' continued Dr Tortoise. 'But if that is so, they are wrong. I have a good job for the right man. For the right man.' Lifting up a shrivelled nose, he closed his eyes, Charles thought completely, but apparently not.

'I see you are not well dressed,' said Tortoise. 'Are you warm enough here?'

'Oh, warm enough, thanks,' replied Charles. Another double whisky would have been nice.

'I will not ask you how you came to your present state, or whether you did anything to deserve it. You are, I presume, a man with little money and with minimal future prospects.'

Charles nodded, and Dr Tortoise went on:

'This room is completely soundproof. The neighbours and the police for that matter, hold me in very high esteem. So, if you report what I say to other authorities, they will believe me, not you. Do you understand?'

Charles breathed a quiet 'Yes.'

'Then listen. I wish you to steal some rings for me from the jewellery shop opposite the cathedral. I have always coveted them, and if you obtain them I will pay you well.

'A crate of whisky and I'll do it,' said Charles.

'Good.' Dr Tortoise stood up and walked behind Charles. He laid two clammy reptilian hands on Charles's shoulders. 'Good. I see that you have little to risk. That is exactly what I want. Will you please stand up?'

Charles stood up. He had no idea why the old man was suddenly so fond of him.

'I imagine you will not mind if I temporarily blindfold you,' the old man said. 'It is regretfully necessary.'

Already he had taken a dark blue scarf (very musty, Charles noticed) and wrapped it around Charles's head. All Charles could see were the little blue patterns of the fabric.

'We are going on a short journey. Indoors, I assure you.' Dr Tortoise took both Charles's hands and led him, like a child, through the gap in the room and down quite a long flight of stairs, Tortoise having first put Charles's right hand on a wooden banister so Charles could use it as he went down.

At the foot of the stairs Tortoise guided Charles to the right, where damp was even heavier in the air. Their footsteps were the only sound, along with Dr Tortoise's long laboured breathing. Suddenly they stopped. Tortoise seemed to be fiddling with something on the wall. There was a minute whoosh of air, and a noise of something sliding. Then the dampness was gone, and they were breathing fresh air. The sliding again, and Charles's blindfold was off.

'Of course you will be wondering where we are,' Dr Tortoise

said, 'but first let me reassure you that you are completely safe.'

'I hope so,' said Charles.

Although his future was nothing to him, there was a natural instinct in him that made dying in summer particularly silly.

Dr Tortoise collapsed into a chair which was tubular and modern, designed in a bright new style like the rest of the room. He continued to breathe in a most uncomfortable-sounding way.

'I do not like it here,' he said. 'The air is too fresh. The conditioners work too well. I look forward to returning to my usual environment. But this room contains the only projector I possess.'

He did not mention that the room was also completely sealed off from the outside world; but Charles felt sure that the room's obvious security was another reason for their visit. For the first time, Charles began to doubt that the old man had invited him down here merely to talk about a possible jewel robbery.

Tortoise beckoned Charles to a seat near him, and then produced another drink, a gin this time, from a snug cabinet inside a wall.

'We are at present directly underneath Canterbury Cathedral,' said Tortoise. Charles managed not to spill his gin. 'Ancient alchemists once had a secret chamber below the tomb of St Thomas. We are in that chamber now. It comes with my house, and only the Archbishop, and the Lord Mayor of the city, know that it is still in use. You now realise, I hope, why you could not be allowed to discover the route here.'

'Don't worry,' said Charles, warming because of the drinks. 'I wouldn't let on.'

'You are wise to say so.'

Tortoise was withdrawing some sort of panel from another cabinet. The room went darker, until all Charles could see was the grey, scaly outline of Tortoise's face against the background of the wall. As the light had dimmed, Charles saw that, just as in the first room, these walls were all covered with photographs of the same person whose photograph was displayed so extensively and repeatedly in the room above. Here the pictures glowed with eerie brightness, and were only visible when the light had gone down.

'Whose picture is it?' asked Charles.

'That is one thing you may not ask me,' Tortoise replied, and his tone was no longer so friendly. 'Do not mention it again.'

Charles resolved not to do so. But it was difficult to avoid noticing that at all times during Tortoise's next speech, the old man's head moved slowly on its sinewy neck, gazing at the walls, and he made little groaning sounds. All of which Charles now respectfully ignored. At least he was warm and there was a good chance of more drink soon. And no-one was calling him a tramp.

Tortoise walked over to the other side of the room. His voice rasped across to Charles and the hundreds of faces shone down.

'I did not send you… ask you here to discuss a jewel robbery. That was merely an attempt to test your worthiness for working for me. Clearly you are prepared to work for me even though a risk may be involved. That is good. I think you will also be able to do a good job for me of the… the matter I propose to explain to you.'

There was a click. A projector had been switched on, and the far wall was flooded with a beam of light. Now, only very faint outlines of the portraits were visible.

Tortoise's voice crackled on.

'Last week, in the French city of Marseilles, a Finnish gentleman died. You will not have heard of it. The news reached no agencies and there was only a very small paragraph in a local paper. The gentleman was old and ugly, he was no loss to the world.'

This last comment was made in a stony cold tone that shivered all through Charles. But he remained as motionless as he could.

'How ugly, you will see for yourself in a moment. I was extremely pleased to hear that this man had died. In life he was a murderous swine, and I hope he will rot and suffer in death. But my joy would be even greater if his friends would also cast off the lives they abuse by eating, breathing and sleeping in an endless succession of miserable days. These are his compatriots, now.'

Another flick, and four large faces appeared on the wall. But what faces! Charles shut his eyes, and only opened them again when Tortoise said, quickly, 'You will get used to the monstrosities in time. I have had these faces taunting me, in memory or in reality, for much of my life.'

When Charles plucked up the courage to look once more, the faces were as ugly and horrible as anything he had ever seen, or imagined. The noses were perched and twisted between the eyes, and the mouths were at hideous angles. Dreadful scar marks had bitten deep into the cheeks and hairline, and none of the faces had any ears. Charles drew in his breath, and finished his gin.

'You will see,' continued Tortoise, 'that these faces are

recognisably those of three men and a woman… The woman is third from the left,' he added. 'Until last week there were five pictures on this slide. These people you see now, these wretched pretences of human beings, are members of a sect. *They* will not call it that, they consider their affiliation to be for the good of the world. But they are a sect nevertheless, a sect of ugliness and lies. They are all Finnish. I have learned to speak their strange language fluently, and they are all old, and their first names, spelled out produce a certain word. Until last week the names were Vilta, Aamu, Lahti, Taivi and Aino. Now only the last four walk this earth, as Vilta is dead.'

'I see. Well, shall I write those names down?' Charles asked. But Tortoise said, no, he had a list prepared and would give it to Charles later.

'All you need to know is that these names spell out the word VALTA. It is a Finnish word, and it means *power*. That, you see, is how they like to think of themselves.'

'I understand,' said Charles. 'But where's the connection with me?'

'I want you to kill them all,' said Tortoise.

'Oh,' said Charles.

5

Helping them along

Charles put down his empty glass.

'Oh no,' he said. 'Sorry, but no way. A little robbery yes, I mean, prison isn't such an awful thing, is it? Prisons are comfortable nowadays. Good food. Even a drink from time to time. But killing people. Oh, no,' he said again.

'A moment,' Tortoise cut in. 'As I said, you are completely free in your choice. If you wish, I shall replace the blindfold, and you can be back on the street in less than ten minutes. Back on the street, back to your poverty, back to your miserable quest for free drinks. Back to being a tramp.'

'Not a tramp,' called Charles. 'Not a tramp.'

'No? Perhaps not. That is not my business.'

'Not a tramp,' Charles said again.

'Very well. Consider this. These people are all old, their deaths are imminent anyway. But so is mine. I am old and I am not well. I cannot carry out this task myself. Before I die, I wish to know that these people are all in their graves, and that can be achieved by… helping them along to their deaths.'

'Helping them along,' repeated Charles.

'Yes,' Tortoise's voice had lost some of its stoniness. 'Pushing them, perhaps apparently accidentally, so that they fall over in a crowded street. Old bones do not mend easily. Perhaps a fright one night. Weak hearts. Two of them are married – the woman called Lahti and the man called Taivi, though their marriage is a desecration of any sanctity in the bonding. They have a daughter, and may be slightly more difficult than the other two. But you are strong. No deliberate assassination is necessary.'

The drinks had warmed Charles. His voice leapt up.

'But isn't that murder, whatever you say? Isn't it? You want me to murder these people!'

'Understand this. I am not asking you to like me, or my ideas. I am asking you to work for me. No personal affection was requested on the postcard. I want you to help four old, ugly, vicious people to their deaths. Argue with your own conscience. If you accept the task, I will provide one European Express credit card and the addresses of the people I want you to kill. When you have fulfilled your objective, I will place fifty thousand English pounds in any bank account you name.'

He looked across to Charles.

'Or I will open one for you. And then place the money in it.'

Charles's brain worked surprisingly rapidly when money was involved, even though it did not have much practice at such speed of calculation. On one side Charles saw himself, pursued by brats, being called a tramp, sinking down until, perhaps he really was one. The other side (always leaping to the future when the 'job' was complete) was rather more attractive. And it was only 'helping along', after all.

Charles gave a nod. 'All right, I'll do it.'

'Good,' said the old man. 'Do you have a passport? You will be going abroad.'

'Yes I do have one somewhere in my bag.'

He did, too, dating from the honeymoon to the Canary

Islands with Betty Stiggs about a year ago, where he had found out the truth. Charles's passport photo looked even more psychotic than passport photos usually do.

'I am glad to hear it,' said Tortoise. 'Had you not had one, I would have supplied you with one.'

'You can do that?' asked Charles.

'Yes, said Tortoise quietly, 'I can do that.' Raising his voice slightly, he added, 'Now, if you open that drawer in the cupboard there on your right, you will find a brown envelope. Inside it is a blank European Express Proconsul credit card - the highest grade of that prestigious card; it cannot be refused anywhere in the world - and the addresses. I will personally pay all the bills you incur on the Proconsul card. Buy whatever is necessary to facilitate your mission and to bring it to a successful conclusion, There are three addresses, as the married couple live together, despite everything. I shall always be available at this address on Cathedral Walk, number 13. You will need to write to me here: I do not have a telephone. You need write to me only if there is any difficulty or if you have any information I need such as that you have made good progress with your mission. When we return to the surface I shall provide you with some rather more suitable clothes.'

Charles did as he was told, opened the envelope, took out the Proconsul card and looked at the addresses. They were all in Marseilles.

'How is your French?' asked Tortoise.

'Who's he?' asked Charles.

'Well, you will no doubt manage satisfactorily with English. I did not expect a knowledge of French, let alone of Finnish. I only wanted someone with a great deal to gain, and little to risk. I have not been disappointed.'

'One thing,' said Charles. 'There's no signature on this Pro… Procon… credit card.'

'Then you must put yours there.' Tortoise had now become very friendly indeed. 'You have my name, now tell me yours, please.'

Charles paused. Suddenly he realised. 'My name,' he said, rather stupidly.

'Yes.'

'It's Charles,' said Charles. 'Charles Edward.'

'Charles Edward what?' asked Tortoise, in a friendly tone.

'Charles Edward Terrapin,' replied Charles. 'Charles Edward Terrapin.'

'Oh,' said Tortoise. He smiled faintly. 'Terrapin. Very well. Perhaps it is auspicious. Perhaps we are a good match. Please sign your name on that white stripe there, and then the card will be yours and yours only.'

Charles didn't know what 'auspicious' meant either, but he decided not to mention that. Using a Canterbury Cathedral ball-point pen the old man lent him, Charles scribbled his signature on the white stripe.

'Well,' said Tortoise, 'I wish you all the best for the successful completion of your mission.'

Marseilles again. That same night. Aino, aged, ugly, Finn, walking home quickly. Eating a piece of bread. Late supper. Goes past a grille in a wall. Hears nothing. A few paces further on coughs, chokes, falls to the road. Hits head on the kerb. Blood everywhere, spurting. Dies. Pity.

It was the second death caused by the previous assassin

Tortoise had used, who had, however, only agreed to kill two of the Finns. Tortoise had seen no reason to tell Charles about the first recruit. Charles was now the only one engaged on the mission.

6

Waking Up

When Charles woke up, he was conscious of two things: 1) he wasn't on a park bench, and 2) the bed on which he was lying had leaked.

Wrong. It wasn't the bed that had leaked. He stumbled onto the carpet, and felt down among the once-pleasant sheets. They were exceedingly damp. Charles Terrapin, armed with the European Express Proconsul card, had done it once more. Two days of utter boozing. Charles's head felt like many of the things that drunken peoples' heads feel like. He staggered vaguely in the direction of the sink and splashed cold water over the top half of his body, then he felt a little better. He pressed a button just above the sink, buzzing the intercom.

'Breakfast, please,' said Charles, feeling important.

'Bananas, orange juice, porridge, bran cereal, cornflakes, bacon and egg, sausage, pineapple segments, what would you like?' crackled a voice back to him.

'No,' called Charles, as loud as his mind allowed him. 'Just milk. Three pints, please. Quick.'

Back on the bed, he replaced the eiderdown and couldn't feel the wetness so much. Perhaps no-one would notice it.

It had been a good two days. About thirty seconds after Tortoise had put him back on the street, Charles was at the nearest bank and had obtained a large cash advance on the credit card. The European Express Proconsul was an international card, *used by an elite group of highly successful people who manage both their business lives and personal lives with professional vigour*, and all the adverts for it had a picture of sleek, glowing, well-dressed people eating at ludicrously expensive restaurants. With great professional vigour, Charles had bought two bottles of gin and had then checked into The Minster, allegedly the best hotel in Canterbury. He left orders at the reception that he wasn't to be disturbed for forty-eight hours. And he wasn't.

Until now. A loud knock on the door.

'Enter,' called Charles, with the lazy indolence that he thought the room service menial would expect. Charles lay very securely on top of the eiderdown on top of the sheets. The boy had a tray with three pints of milk and a little glass which he left by Charles's bed.

'Thank you.' The words swayed and fell from Charles's mouth.

The boy waited.

'Thank you.' Once more.

'I brought yer breakfast,' the young waif uttered, fixing his eyes firmly on (so Charles thought) the wet sheets.

'Well done!' said Charles.

The boy said nothing, only looked.

'Well,' said Charles, 'I'm sure you have a lot to do.'

''Aven't I?' the waif was less helpful-sounding.

They both looked at each other.

'Get out, you little prat!' yelled Charles. The boy, who obviously expected guests to reach for their wallets at this point, was somewhat taken aback by Charles's cry. He was out of the door in an instant. Running down the stairs he called out to Maggie, a nearby chambermaid, that 'The bloke in number twenty-eight is as tight as a gnat's arse,' before scampering to the room service kitchen to find out who was his next victim.

After drinking two pints of milk, Charles felt much better, and even gave a few thoughts to the reason why he had received Tortoise's card. The old man's envelope was lying screwed up in a sock beneath the bed. Charles pressed it into shape and studied the addresses. Now and then his distorted vision coincided sufficiently to make out a few words. Marseilles, that was clear enough. And since there would be wine in Marseilles, and maybe women, and since the past was not to be mentioned, and since (after all) he had promised a feeble old man that he would help him, Charles resolved that he would, in fact, go to Marseilles. The future was spread out, waiting, like a large cowpat.

Charles packed his things in his bag, including the remaining bottle of gin and pint of milk. In a few minutes he was ready.

Maggie finished the room next door and moved to open Charles's room.

Charles packed the last thing (a bottle opener) and moved to the door. Maggie knocked on it.

'Just going,' he explained, and slipped by.

Maggie was in the room for several minutes before she turned her attention to the sheets.

But it was all right, because Charles found a cab outside and in two hours was at London's Gatwick airport. Another flash of the Proconsul card and he had a ticket. And an hour later he was high over then English Channel, with the hangover slowly being replaced by travel sickness. It was hot, as it had been for the past three weeks, but even hotter in Marseilles.

'Old bones do not mend easily. Weak hearts.' These phrases, written in characters that could have been traced by a tarantula with delirium tremens, lay like a short suicide note on a beer-mat beside Charles. It was just after lunchtime in Marseilles, with the sun flaring nightmarish rays over the city, and with most of the sensible natives asleep under fans or rolling over each other in siesta-time sexual stupors. Charles, on a sunny table in one of the city's most touristy cafes, was demonstrating that not only mad dogs and Englishmen, but also reptiles, stay out in the midday sun.

As he stared dreamily along the empty streets and into the vacuity of his own mind, those two phrases of Dr Tortoise swirled around in him to such an extent that he needed to write them down before they would go away. It was the sun, and the delayed effects of the Canterbury drinks. So, there was a job to do and a reward at the end. But when Charles thought of the actual problem involved in finding the victims and then 'helping them along' he preferred to sit in the sun and do nothing. Tomorrow could wait. And all the first week of his stay in Marseilles he walked by the Mediterranean Sea in the morning, sat in the café when the sun rose, and slept luxurious hours at his hotel by night. The problem of What To Do Next was covering his life with apathy. But he was considering the problem carefully. No need to make silly mistakes. Talking of which…

7

Englishmen abroad

'You English?'

'Me?'

'Well, I wasn't exactly talking to your cup of coffee, deary. Help me in, will you? Much too small, these damned chairs!'

A monstrously fat man had come to Charles's table and Charles held the wicker chair steady as the new arrival squeezed a mighty bottom into place. His backside was so large it squelched and squeezed all over the seat, as if bits of it might fall onto the floor.

'Mind if I sit down?' asked the fat man, after he had sat down. Charles opened his hands in a gesture of easy-goingness, and the man ordered a Martini Bianco with ice and a cherry.

'I can always tell, you know. Always recognise the English. An Englishman has a way of sitting, you know, that puts him above the average foreigner.'

It was late afternoon, when the native population had begun work again after the searing heat of the sun, a week after Charles had arrived in Marseilles. The week had gone by as uneventfully as most of Charles's life. He had sat in the café, drinking coffee and thinking about what he should do. Sitting, looking into the distance, trying to get his brain to form a plan. An unopened copy of *French in Ten Relatively Painless Days* was by his side.

Charles's new friend extended a great fat hand, that was sweaty and stained with nicotine. Charles shook it rather gingerly.

'Scales,' said the man. 'Erasmus Scales is the name. Known all over Marseilles. Scales. Befriender of the Englishman.'

Dipping into his cavernous blue blazer, he took out some grimy business cards and after inspecting a few, handed one to Charles. Charles read *Erasmus Scales, 113 ruelle de merde, Marseilles, France, Dealer in tropical hides and pelts.*

'That's me,' said Scales, unnecessarily. 'This is my English-language card. Until recently we did most of our trade in crocodile skins, actually, but since the damned government put a restriction out, we've had to make up what we can with armadillo hides.'

The waiter brought Scales's drink. Charles said, 'So do you know all the English here?'

'Never said that, old boy. Not all of them. There are one or two English here, not many mind, who I would prefer *not* to know. But otherwise, yes. Keeps me sane, you know, talking to Englishmen. With that and my copy of *The Daily Squalor* I manage quite well. Always said, Marseilles is a good place if you can forget the smells. You know, I once met a Frenchman here who said he took a shower twice a year. On Bastille Day and on his wife's birthday. Typical.'

In one suck of his pendulous, saliva-dripping lips the Martini Bianco and ice and cherry vanished into the unmapped portals of Erasmus Scales's body.

'Been here long?' asked Scales, after he had wiped his hand over his mouth and belched.

'Only a week. Don't really know the place yet.'

'What are you doing here?'

Clearly, Charles thought, Englishmen abroad did not bother with the usual formalities of getting to be intimate with someone. In fact, one of the very few constructive things Charles had done in his short time in the city was to prepare an answer to just this question.

'Well, in fact, I'm working for a charity.'

'A charity?' Scales's entire body rippled with the shock of this answer. 'You mean you're not in business for yourself, deary?'

'No,' said Charles, wishing Scales wouldn't call him that. 'I'm working for a charity that tries to persuade older people to come out of their houses and walk in the fresh air. In fact, I'm working on a few cases at this moment.'

Bewildered though he was by Charles's unselfish pursuits, Scales found the idea rather interesting compared to *his* daily work, which consisted of paying illiterate and starving Africans extortionately low prices for the hides they brought to him.

'Who are the cases?' asked Scales.

'If you must know,' said Charles, 'you can see. I have their pictures.'

He took out the slides of the four remaining Finns which Tortoise had put in the projector, showed them to Scales who, lifting the slides up to the sunlight, immediately dropped his jaw in amazement.

'So ugly!' he exclaimed. 'So damned ugly! French I expect?'

'No,' said Charles. 'Actually, they're Finnish.'

'I see,' returned Scales. 'Interesting.' Scales was studying the fourth slide, that of the Finn called Aino.

'Tell you what, deary,' he said. 'I've *seen* that face somewhere before. Wouldn't get it wrong, would you? Not with a face as horrible as that.'

Charles thought Aino's face was pretty bad, but not much worse than Scales's heavy jowls and dark, chaffed nose. Scales clicked his fingers and a waiter swayed over to him like a ballerina. Scales said something to the waiter in French which Charles didn't quite catch.

'I ordered a local paper,' said Scales. 'Want to have a look at something, old boy.'

The waiter soon brought a copy of *Ici à Marseille* which came out every week. Scales eagerly thumbed his great fingers through it, leaving, Charles noticed, a damp stain on all the pages he touched.

'Here,' said Scales excitedly. 'Look here, deary!'

There was a small picture of Aino's revolting-looking face about halfway down the page. Scales's eyes quickly scanned the accompanying story.

'Well,' said Scales, pushing the paper towards Charles. '*He* won't be needing any of your charity.'

'Where?' asked Charles, after trying to find the writing to go with the picture. 'I don't quite… follow… all of these words.'

Scales got the message.

'It's in French,' he said, loudly. 'I shouldn't worry, old boy. I only learnt the damned language because I have to deal with these crooked local traders. I always say, if it's not said in English, it's not worth saying.'

So he translated the story for Charles. It said that this man, Aino, had been found dead, of an apparent heart attack, in a street near the centre of the city. It mentioned also that he had been eating a piece of bread at the time, and that doctors believed the heart attack was brought on by choking on the bread.

'Well,' said Charles. 'I'm jolly glad I met you.' He took out a piece of paper from his other pocket on which there was a list.

~~VILTA~~
AAMU
LAHTI
TAIVI
AINO

Charles had already crossed out the first name, as Tortoise had said he had been killed about a week before he, Charles, had come for the job. Now, feeling that the fifty thousand was already in his grasp, he carefully etched out the last name on the list. Scales watched all this with great interest.

'Tell you what, old boy,' he said, after Charles had finished his literary task, 'How would you like a spot of help? I'm not very busy at this very moment and my office-boy does most of the... er, transactions. To tell you the truth, I wouldn't mind hearing a bit about old England. You say you've only been away a week? I haven't been back since the queen was crowned.'

At this point, obviously honouring his recent regal reference, Scales eased himself out of his chair and stood up.

'I don't know,' said Charles. 'In the years I've worked for this charity' - he thought he said that quite well - 'I've always worked by myself.'

'Come on, old boy,' said Scales. 'We English ought to stick together. In any case,' he added, 'I speak a little Finnish. Learnt it up north after the war, when we were selling reindeer hide.'

'Oh,' said Charles. 'That's a bit different.' He didn't say that the problem of how he was going to talk to the Finns had been an issue of great concern to him since his coming to Marseilles.

'Perhaps you could help me.'

'Worth a try, old boy,' said Erasmus Scales.

Charles now stood up, and Scales paid the bill in a massive flurry of banknotes and condescension.

'Well,' said Scales, as they were walking towards the Old Port, where Scales had promised to show Charles his office, 'which of the blighters is first?'

Three left. Charles decided it was best to start with the one who was by himself. He took out a slide, and showed it to Scales. A trolley bus, flaring sparks under the electric wires, rattled round the corner.

'Aamu,' said Charles.

8

Milk necessary again

But they didn't start on their mission for two days. It turned out that Scales, like his new friend, was extremely partial to satisfying his thirst, and that the best way to appease this mighty human desire was, in Scales's opinion, a sweet fortified wine that could be obtained from a merchant Scales knew who had a shop near the Old Port. Its sweetness, that went some way towards concealing its strength, was the reason why, forty-eight hours after meeting, Charles and Scales were lying groaning, in the salon that adjoined Scales's office on ruelle de merde.

Charles was the first to wake up, having had rather more experience in this sort of thing than his new compatriot. He had only a very hazy memory of the past hours, but one thing stood out clearly. He remembered some stairs, and a door with name tabs on it in scrawled black on white next to buttons, then Charles rang a bell. Charles also remembered a woman opening the door, staring at himself and Scales, who had his fat right hand full of 100-franc notes, and the woman shrieking and banging the door shut. Then a loud rattling sound behind the door, as if it were being barricaded or something.

After both the men were awake, and after Charles, with a haste borne of long practice, had ordered some milk from a nearby shop to flush out their hangovers, and after Scales had been sick, and after Scales had said that he now felt damned good, and that a day on the booze tended to clear the system and refresh the brain, and after he had been sick again and said that he wished he hadn't said that, Scales took out a map of the streets of Marseilles and together they found where Aamu lived. Scales wanted to take a taxi, but Charles said no, people working for the charity always walked. So they walked.

It was the moment Charles Edward Terrapin had been waiting for. Scales, with the noonday heat streaming sweat from his huge head, had rung the doorbell where Aamu was supposed to live. For a long time there was no answer. Then a padding of feet could be heard on the other side of the door, then a rattle, and Charles drew his breath. Now, at last, they would come face to face, in the flesh, with the horror which had haunted Charles ever since he had seen the slides in Tortoise's underground den!

But it was only the housemaid.

'The Finnish gentleman has a flat upstairs,' she said to Scales in French, after he had asked her, in an accent that would have made a Linguaphone record bend and shatter, where '*l'homme finlandais*' lived. So they went up a long, dusty flight of stairs which smelt as if they had not been aired since they had been built, presumably sometime the previous century. Finally, when Scales was producing perspiration in a quantity that made Charles feel a bit scared, they reached the top. There was a tiny little door to the left with *Aamu* written in long copperplate handwriting, followed by a rather long surname which neither of them bothered to look at. Scales drew a few breaths that must have reduced the oxygen content on the landing by about fifty percent, then he knocked loudly at the door. About five minutes later, when both of them were about to go, it opened.

What surprised Charles most of all on seeing Aamu for the very first time was that, in spite of everything, the Finn was not as ugly as he had expected. He certainly had an extremely disfigured face, with a tiny shrivelled nose and no ears, and a mouth at a wrong angle and deep scars. But Aamu was a bent-over old man, tiny and aged, with very white hair nestling on the top of his head, and a stoop that made Charles feel an emotion rather more like sympathy than repugnance. He awoke from such a humanitarian feeling when he realised that, as part of the deal to receive the much-anticipated fifty thousand pounds, he had got to *help* this old man to his death. Well, it had to be done.

'Yes, yes, yes,' said Scales to Aamu in Finnish, nodding his head furiously at Aamu, and it was certainly true of Scales that what he lacked in linguistic skills, which was plenty, he made up for in violent gesture. He turned to Charles, who had no idea what Scales was saying.

'Listen, deary. I told you you could rely on old Erasmus. No problem. He's a tough customer, but I'll do it. I'm making him think we're doing him a favour. I'm making the blighter think we're really good people.'

That must be difficult, thought Charles, who occasionally had blinding bursts of self-insight. But apparently Scales was doing his job quite well, for the little old Finnish gentleman put out a small and shrunken finger and beckoned them both inside. The door shut behind Charles as he walked, cautiously, into Aamu's abode.

It reminded him of Tortoise's rooms. The walls were not

covered in portraits in the regular and methodical fashion of Charles's hopefully future financier, but instead Aamu had three large paintings hanging on each wall. They were paintings of younger people, of very beautiful, clean-looking people. Some of the paintings were of people playing in the snow, and some were close-up portraits of a couple, or perhaps a man and woman by themselves, looking thoughtfully into the distance. There was not a single blemish on any of the faces, with even, very white teeth and, especially as far as the women were concerned, high, delicate cheekbones. In such a dirty and grubby little room the pictures, which Charles noticed looked very clean and polished, seemed out of place – one expected to see scruffy landscapes on the walls, not such large beautiful paintings. Scales took Charles's arm and directed him to a seat that Aamu had indicated. The Finn and Scales went on talking for a little while.

'Blighter wants to see your identity card,' said Scales, turning back to Charles. 'You got one?'

'Identity card? Of course not. They don't have them in England.'

'Well, show him anything,' said Scales.

So Charles took out his precious Proconsul credit card and with professional vigour thrust it at Scales. The fat man engulfed it in a large fist and handed it to the Finn. They talked on a bit more. Aamu handed the card back.

'He wants to know where you want to take him,' said Scales.

'There's a lovely walk by the ocean,' said Charles, after a few moments' evil thinking. 'Beautiful view of the sea, and the air there is *so* fresh and good.'

There was another pause, and another burst of bubbling,

weird-sounding Finnish speech between the two men. Then Scales turned towards Charles, his fat many-faceted belly bouncing with pride.

'I've damn well done it,' he called, in a fine, boastful tone. 'He's coming. Says it's very nice of us. Only he wants a glass of gin on the way. Rules allow that, I expect?'

Charles's heart beat faster. Fifty thousand pounds.

Lying on a promontory that curves back to the coast of Provence, Marseilles contains hundreds of little beaches within its territory, as well as three massive hills that touch the clouds on overcast days. A short distance out to sea is the island of If, with the fabled Château d'If, and all around it blue, warm sea, where the waves twinkle like jewels as the sun hits them. On the day when Scales and Charles led out an old memory-charged man for a walk by the ocean, the sea was still, serene and dark blue, and the sun on the cliff tops was hot. It was too alive a day for death.

Which may have been the reason why, as the three men walked slowly along the coastal path, Aamu between them and Scales nearest the sea, Charles, who had been very peaceful a few moments before, cried out 'My legs!' and threw himself headlong at Aamu, intending to knock the Finn off the cliff side but only succeeding in falling over himself, though not quite, gripping onto a tuft of grass and yelling 'help', as he looked for a moment below and saw the dreadful gap and seagulls flying beneath him. Scales grabbed his wrists just in time because the grass was coming away at its roots, saying, 'Don't worry old boy,' and used his great fat, sweaty, dripping bulk to lift Charles clear of the fall as Aamu looked on very shocked and

Scales heaved Charles onto the firmer grass where Charles lay panting and alive. Scales couldn't believe what had happened but thought the sun had got to him.

Back in the flat, Scales watched anxiously over the still trembling body of his fellow countryman as Aamu, shaken but much the better for his brisk and exciting walk, prepared coffee. While the Finn was pottering around in the kitchen, Scales, peering down through his pig-like eyes enmeshed by fat, shook his head and said:

'Listen, old boy. You damn near got yourself killed just then. Would have done if Erasmus hadn't been to hand. Aren't you a bit *keen* my boy? A bit enthusiastic for the old devil? I mean, charity is charity, but he's a foreigner. No point you wearing yourself out and then fainting on the job is there?'

As Charles listened to this speech, the single thought haunting his base mind was that at least Scales had not twigged his, Charles's, real purpose in meeting Aamu. Indeed, the fat fool was even being sympathetic. Charles felt that the best thing to do was to lie still and look frightened. Which he did. Scales, firmly plumped in Aamu's armchair, drank his coffee and wiped the smears that dribbled down his chin.

Aamu was as pleased as a shrivelled and disfigured old man can be. As he served coffee, strong and in porcelain cups, he babbled high-pitched, tumbling Finnish to Scales.

'The blighter says he's very happy we took him for such a beautiful walk,' the fat man interpreted. Charles, still pretending to be comatose, couldn't believe it.

Aamu went on.

'And he says he wants to invite us to dinner next week,' Scales informed Charles. 'It's a Finnish holiday and he says he'd love to have some company.'

Charles opened his eyes. He gazed around the room. At the fat bulk of Scales, suspended over him like a side of beef, and then at the walls. At the pictures, the pictures of happy life, of young Finns playing, gambolling in the snow. Clean faces, white hair, unblemished skins.

Tortoise's voice: 'Old bones do not mend easily. Weak hearts.'

Weak hearts.

Aamu had cooked a fine dinner, in the true Finnish style. There was a great bowl in the middle of the table, full of something Aamu called *glögg*. It was steaming and giving off a wonderful smell of cinnamon and delicate wines. Scales sniffed it, drawing in great inhalations of oxygen, nitrogen and burnt wine. His body gave forth anticipatory moisture from the pores and his perverse hormone balance changed as he prepared for feeding time. From the kitchen came a curious aroma of some kind of meat.

'*Poro*,' explained Aamu to Scales, and the old man put his hands to his head for antlers.

'Ah,' said Scales, breathing heavily and perspiring, 'Reindeer.'

'*Kyllä*,' said Aamu.

Charles had not yet arrived.

When Charles was half an hour late Aamu pleaded with Scales to start the meal. The reindeer, the *poro*, had been shipped directly from Helsinki and if it was not eaten now would taste terrible.

Scales listened to his pleadings without taking much notice. Of course it was absurd that an Englishman should be deprived of his dinner just because this little Finn was getting nervous.

But the reindeer smelt very good. Torn between patriotism and bestial hunger, Scales's stomach got the better of his prejudice.

'All right,' he said to Aamu, in French. 'Fetch it.'

Aamu didn't move.

Then Scales said it in Finnish and Aamu hobbled joyfully to the kitchen. Scales thought, as he adjusted his napkin down the front of his trousers, that he would save some for Charles. But the reindeer meat looked as delectable as it smelt, and was speared with delicious tiny purple berries. An hour later, after Scales had gorged himself like a dinosaur, they put down their knives and forks, and Aamu (who had eaten almost nothing in his haste to give his much-loved guest as much as possible) brought out a ladle. The strong, intensely alcoholic *glögg* lay steaming like a volcano. And when *that* was all gone, Scales sat back in his seat and let out a belch that would have taken Jericho. In Scales's drunken mind, the images of the young Finns rotated clockwise and then anti-clockwise like a speeding propeller. So Scales sat and breathed as Aamu went to the lavatory.

Charles was waiting for him. Weak hearts. Tortoise had used a projector, so Charles would use one too. He had taken the electric light bulb away and instead fitted one he had made himself. There was a fiendish face carved in plastic on one side, the face of a devil. Aamu would see it and have a heart attack. So easy.

Charles was thinking, as he was waiting for Aamu to come to the lavatory, how good it was that Scales never used a toilet because of his artificial bladder. He even thought that Scales deserved perhaps a few hundred pounds for his help.

Aamu flicked the switch. On the far side of the room he could make out a sort of black thing. But the Finn was drunk, and he could not see much at the best of times. Charles, failed grocer, failed housebreaker, failed husband, failed assassin.

There was a clatter. Charles had fallen down from his hiding place behind the immersion heater.

'*Mitä*?' Aamu asked in amazement as he saw Charles. '*What?*' But the answer never came. Aamu was out of the room before Charles knew it. The Finn had known such deeds before. In the past. He ran to his bedroom.

'What's that damned row?' Scales arrived on the scene, his body as drunk as his brain. In the lavatory, he was wedged in the door. Then he saw Charles. 'Old boy...' and Scales's mouth dropped open, the lower lip reaching further down than ever before. Should he embrace his compatriot, or ask him what the hell he was doing there and why hadn't he come for the meal?

'Quick!' cried Charles. 'That Finn - where's he gone? What's he fetching?'

'No idea,' blabbered Scales as Charles moved nearer. Scales was strong, but he was drunk. Charles was sober for once.

Enter Aamu. The past was flying back more every second. He was no longer an aged, utterly lonely man, haunted, tortured, made insane by his memories. By his pictures. By the puckish wonderful girl of his past, when he was young. The muscles were filling out, the face was back to normal. Strong, alert, loving and living. Aamu had a black revolver in his right hand and pointed the gun at Charles. His finger closed on the trigger. This intruder must die. A trick! But what else could he, Aamu, old man and shrivelled, have expected, in the end?

Then Scales fell. He fell heavily, stunned by drink, by food, by shock. He fell onto the Finn, and the gun rolled into the room and bounced off the cistern. *This was it*, the thought hammered into Charles. No more waiting. Get out of this if you can. Two enemies on the floor, fifty thousand pounds. Certain failure if caught. Failure. A tramp.

He picked the gun up from the floor. It felt cold. Cold and old and surprisingly heavy.

Charles fired at Aamu. A mighty crash. Had he done it? Had he really fired a gun? Charles had half expected the thing to be full of blanks, or even to produce a little strip of paper saying BANG.

But that hadn't happened. Where Aamu lay, blood was already welling from his chest. Charles's bullet had burst the heart, and Aamu's heart had gone long before.

'Old boy. Old boy. England!' cried Scales. His brain beat furiously and he made one leap for Charles. But the gun had gone off once, and so Charles was used to killing now. Doing it again was no problem. Charles pulled off a few more shots at Scales. They spat into Scales's fat body and carved slices through the about to be ex hide-dealer.

The noise of the shells was appalling, and Charles felt insane. He fired a final shot at Scales and then the revolver was empty and the trigger clicked against empty chambers. The fat man was looking like one of those Swiss cheeses with gaps everywhere. Only, not quite so funny.

Aamu was dead. Scales was near it and getting nearer. Then Charles was dashing, rushing through the hot evening, running to Marseilles central railway station. Soon he was on a train, and cutting through the night, He spent the next day under a bush, far away from any people, hiding, clothes torn.

Very hungry, looking like a murderer, looking like a fugitive. Looking like a tramp.

9

The black tender

The small car stopped on a nearby grass verge.

'Wanna lift?' called a girl's American-accented voice from the passenger seat window. 'Get a move on, it's too hot to stop.'

Rod ran, flailing legs and arms. 'Where you going?' he asked as he reached the car.

'Who cares? Just get in.'

Rod got in, the door slammed shut, and they revved off. The car's engine made a deafening screech, but Rod yelled above it. 'Hey, thanks for the lift. I've been scraping the tar two hours. Nothing.'

'We only give lifts to the right bloke,' called back the girl, obviously steeped in the slang of the road. 'Soon as we saw ya, Beryl and I, we knew you was going to be a good lift. Your gear told us that.'

'I'm heading south,' said Rod. 'Trying to get to the South of France.'

'Now ain't that a coincidence,' the driver, Beryl, spoke this time. ''Cause we are too.'

'How far down, dabs?'asked Rod, glad they understood him a little.

'Mon-ak-ko,' said Beryl. 'Where the sun is.'

'And the men,' said her companion.

'Those as well,' said Beryl. She paused a moment and glanced at Rod in the rear view mirror. 'Since we're all gonna be moving together, what's your name?'

'Coaster, call me Coaster,' replied Rod immediately. He preferred his surname to his first name when he was travelling.

'Coaster, eh?' said Beryl. 'Cream name. Cream, don't you think, Bernice?'

'I'd say,' said the other girl. 'Where'd you get a name like that, eh, Coaster?'

'On the road,' said Rod casually. 'It sort of happened.'

'Great,' and Beryl looked at Rod in the mirror once more.

'My, you are cream, aren't you? I'm Beryl and this here's Bernice. We're from the U.S. of A.'

'Where?' asked Rod.

'Marytown,' said Beryl vaguely. 'But we're travelling now. Had enough of the old country. Oh yeah, that we have.'

'You bet,' said Bernice and Rod looked out of the window. A couple of dabs were trying to thumb a lift, using large smiles. They whizzed by, as did hundreds of other cars, like contestants in a constantly place-changing Grand Prix.

Rod's self-inflicted celibacy was now two weeks old, and he was already feeling the pangs. There were times, when he saw a dab and saw that the dab saw him, when he wondered what he was doing. Only the thought of the Mexican bead-seller kept him going. But the mornings were getting better. When early light came he felt stronger, ready for activity, not just sleep. The bad side of it was a funny feeling in the pit of his stomach and being more on edge. But he was free, and he was scraping the tar: hitchhiking, which he always loved to do. There were all the good sides of scraping the tar; the early mornings by the roadside, not knowing what was going to happen, expecting everything. Meals at night in deserted motorway cafes where the idle waiters took pity on him and gave him free chips. Good talk in cars, fresh air, and a different place to sleep every night. But no slozes.

Bernice embarked on a long, boring anecdote involving a donkey and a drunken saloon keeper, which gave Rod a chance to think about what he was going to do. One of the lifts since Calais had been with a strange, lanky Dutch throb who had given him a lift and also let him have the address of a *kind off commune*, as the Dutch throb put it, saying *off* instead of *of*, in the hills north of Nice, where you could live from *what you got on the land* and where it was even actually quite easy to avoid a sloz, if you didn't want one. The Dutch throb had spoken warmly of each member of the commune having their own little cave in the dusty hillside, and Rod liked that idea. So he thought meeting Bernice and Beryl was very fortunate. Having spent a few days at some towns, Rod was now only about half way on his journey. Lyons was the next big city.

As Bernice finished her anecdote it occurred to Rod that she had been looking at him in a funny way for quite some time; she had been sneaking little glances through the mirror. But he didn't think much about it, because who cared as long as they were going where he wanted, but also because the ways of men and women are complicated, and Rod had been away from studying these ways for two weeks, so he was already a bit rusty. But about five minutes afterwards Rod was rather surprised when Beryl pulled off the main motorway and onto a slip road, and then about half a mile along a dirty country lane that was overgrown with hedge and strewn with bits of paper and apple cores.

It was an extremely hot afternoon, and even hotter in the car. 'Just need a rest,' Beryl explained, pulling her window down.

'Fine,' said Rod, and he opened the door and took out his scissors to trim his toe nails. A small lizard, which had been basking on a stone, leapt away into the thicket, leaving a minute trail of slime behind. After the din of the car, the lane, with the sun beating down upon them, was most pleasantly silent, and Rod smiled to himself as he cut at his big toe, on which stood a large horny nail.

Casually, clicking her fingers together, Bernice came round to the other side of the car, to where Rod had opened the door.

'Hi,' she said, her voice rippling above the silence. 'Hot, ain't it?'

'You bet,' said Rod, and he nodded slightly. The nail was going to take some prising.

'You wanna loosen that gear?' asked Bernice. 'I mean, it's cream gear, but… is that really camel skin?'

'Yeah,' said Rod, but he wasn't really listening. Cutting your toenails was difficult if someone stood in the light.

'I can tell,' said Bernice, getting nearer. 'It's the smell.'

A final snip and the big toenail was off. And Bernice's arms were around his head.

'Forget about them toes,' she said, but Rod had pushed her away before she'd finished.

'So what you doing, dab?' he yelled as he stood up. 'What's the big idea, eh?'

'Whaddya mean what's the big idea?' Bernice had dropped back and was staring at him as if he had a face like Aamu's.

'You're a throb, I'm a dab, *that's* the big idea.'

'I thought this was a lift.' Rod had put on his shoes and socks and zipped the scissors away.

Beryl, who so far had just sat in the driver's seat and watched him, now said. 'A lift. A lift? Listen, honey, when we pick up men we reckon they're men. Not fags.'

'And it's hot,' said Bernice, as if this fact was the ultimate point Rod had missed. 'And you say you just want a lift?'

'So maybe you don't like women,' Beryl said.

'Or maybe he swings both ways,' called Bernice, who was fastening her bra back into position.

'Yeah, men and boys,' Beryl said.

'Listen dabs, listen dabs,' and for the first time in his life Rod was stuck for something good to say to a girl. 'You know how it is, I'm scraping the tar, travellin' around. I don't want a sloz, not right now.'

'Nor anytime, I reckon,' said Beryl.

'We oughtta have had beards,' said Bernice.

'And splicers,' chorused Beryl.

Rod was looking at them both through Beryl's window now. They were obviously both totally annoyed with him. Bernice wasn't even looking at him, and Beryl gave him a rather nasty glare. Bernice lifted Rod's rucksack from the back seat and toppled it into the lane.

'We're off to get a man,' snarled Beryl. 'If we find any fags, we'll let ya know.'

The car revved up again, and Beryl turned it in a tyre-screeching turn. Then they were off, churning oil and muck from the exhaust pipe, down the lane. Rod watched the car until it turned back onto the main road.

It was curiously quiet. The grass and hedges were scorched yellow by the sun, and from their midst the twinkling piping of crickets leapt up. Far in the distance Rod could hear a quiet hum spinning across the motorway. The silence was something to listen to. It seemed to Rod that he had never heard silence before and he listened very hard. If you paid a great deal of attention, it was even possible to distinguish certain crickets' chirpings from others. So walked some way from the main road, then sat down on the hard, dusty ground under a sun that poured heat down in a massive all-embracing explosion, and Rod listened to the crickets. His rucksack lay unused and still beside him, like a great dangerous bomb.

The sun slowly crept towards the horizon, the crickets' cries had already diminished, but still Rod sat his posture. Though now his eyes were closed, and he was listening to nothing but the blood beating inside his brain.

But the changing smells of evening and the encroaching darkness woke him up. He decided to go back to scrapong the tar. He thought that if he could get a reasonably long lift, he could have a good snooze in the back seat. Then he noticed a battery of lights about half a mile away down the road, and Rod thought he might as well get to what he supposed was a service station. He knew they were easy places to hitch from, as drivers were usually in a good mood after their meal, and besides they would be driving slowly as they came towards the motorway again and could easily see him.

But when Rod reached the large complex, which doubled as a petrol station and also as a restaurant the first thing he saw was a great collection of green French police cars, and a constant supply of *gendarmerie* toppling out of them and marching up the steps towards the café. Rod wondered what was going on. As he looked, policemen emerged in twos or threes, each little group with a struggling person between them. The police bundled their charges into a large van that stood outside and then went up the steps again, presumably to look for some more.

Rod was about a hundred yards from where it was all happening. 'Do not go any nearer,' a voice said beside him, that of a middle-aged rather cute-looking woman with short brown hair and a duffle-coat buttoned up to her neck against the chilly night air.

'My son is travelling in England,' she said in English, in a French accent. 'My son also has a rucksack, so I 'ave sympathy with you. I saw your British flag on the rucksack. I hate to think what is going to happen to those young people up there. I am sure very few of them can have done anything wrong.'

The lady beckoned to Rod and he followed her finger to where she pointed out a shaded spot by a large tree. 'No-one shall see you here,' she said. 'And if you go any nearer you shall certainly be arrested.'

'What for?' asked Rod.

'Oh, they will think of something.'

'Wow,' said Rod, then wondered what term he could use to address this woman. Certainly 'dab' wouldn't do. 'What's the bean, then?'

'I am sorry,' said the woman, 'I do not understand you.'

'Sorry. What's happening?'

'It is drugs. The local police have decided that all people who look as if they might sell drugs… which means in essence whoever the police choose… must be arrested and examined.

It happens every six months or so.'

'Oh,' said Rod, 'so this lot are going off to prison?'

'Almost certainly, yes. They *will* come out. But when they do come out they will not have their rucksacks.'

Rod watched as the police fetched out about twenty more young people, and then they had them all apparently, for the cars and the vans started up and disappeared along the motorway entry road. When the noise had gone, Rod turned round to thank the woman, but she was gone.

'I'll yawn the mud here,' Rod said to himself, and he prepared to do so underneath the tree. The ground beneath looked fairly comfortable. Certainly, it would not be a good idea to go to the café, not tonight. Never knew what might be lurking about.

A torch beam shone on him. A policeman appeared silhouetted by the light. He called to Rod, something loud in French, Rod didn't move.

'English?' asked the man sharply.

Rod nodded.

'You will wait here, not move.'

The policeman took out his walkie-talkie and spoke into it. Rod wasn't sure what the policeman was saying, but he was pretty sure that the throb wasn't radioing home to ask his mother what was for dinner.

'Have you any narcotics about you?' asked the policeman.

'No,' said Rod, which was true, but even as he said it he glanced about him. The café, a hundred yards away and up some steps. Behind him, the road back to the motorway going south. Grass to the left, and a large car park to the right.

Rod chose the car park. One good thing that all his slozes had given him was strength. Strength in the legs, where it counted. While the policeman was still fiddling with the tuning knob on his radio Rod had slung the rucksack around one shoulder and was already five paces away. But the other guy was a policeman. He drew his gun and pointed it towards Rod.

'Halt!' he yelled.

But Rod didn't, and the policeman knew he could never shoot at a young guy, even if he might have been a drugs pusher. So the policeman (whose name was Jean-Pierre Wapping, his father having emigrated to France twenty-five years before) gave chase.

Rod swerved behind an articulated lorry, but Wapping saw him at once and Rod ran towards the darkness at the back of the car park. The rucksack was very heavy, and whenever he ran it bounced up and down into his back and hurt like mad, but not as much as being in a French prison would hurt. He saw at once that there were only two choices: try and make for the cover, about thirty yards away, of the long black tender of a lorry. or go for the trees. Trees. Tender. Tender, trees. No way of knowing which was the best one. Rod was tiring now, while Wapping was only getting into the swing of things. No point prolonging the agony.

Rod made his choice in light a little too black for Wapping to see clearly. By the time the Frenchman's eyes were sharp again Rod had vanished. Trees. tender. Tender, trees. Wapping remembered hearing that the English loved the countryside. He made for the trees, waving his torch around him like a scythe.

Rod was crouching by the tender when he saw Wapping disappear into the thicket. Rod knew that when Wapping found he wasn't there he'd go for the second possibility. Hiding by the tender wouldn't do.

There was no time to notice whether there was anybody in the cab. The tender was pretty massive; it stretched for a good thirty feet, or maybe more. Rod rushed to the back, and felt the door handle. He gave it a tug. It pulled down. *Thank God it's not locked*, Rod thought. With pretty much his last piece of strength, Rod chucked his rucksack into the tender, and scrambled inside himself. He closed the door very carefully and quietly, then lay down inside the tender, panting.

He was safe, at least from Jean-Pierre Wapping.

Wapping had found nothing, and he was hungry. It was also very dark. After all, only one of them had got away. He radioed base and said that he would be back in ten minutes. Then he went to a public telephone and rang his mother. 'What is there for dinner?' he asked.

'Cassoulet,' she said.

'*Formidable*, my favourite,' said Wapping. He was happy.

It was probably morning, although there was no way of being certain. When Rod awoke the rucksack was still pushing down on his back and tender was moving. Rod got up and put the rucksack by his side. For the first time he looked round to see where he was.

The tender was even bigger than he thought, and completely windowless. The only reason he could see at all was that at the front of the tender there was a feeble light which cast its faint glow all over the area, leaving strange-looking shadows in corners. Tired as he was, the shadows seemed to him like ghosts. Rod couldn't see exactly where the light came from,. The tender seemed to be full mostly of old junk, chairs, tables, cloths draped over other pieces of furniture, and with several rolled-up carpets on the floor. He could perhaps have picked a path out by all this stuff if he had wanted to, but the effort was too much at present. He sat down again and thought about Bernice and Beryl, and how, a few weeks earlier, what happened wouldn't have happened.

He was aroused from this rather reverie by a creepy, scary, groaning noise.

'What's the bean?' Rod called out softly, urgently. Then he remembered the fate of that remark last time and substituted, 'What's happening, who are you?'

'H…e…l…p,' produced a groany voice from behind a pile of suitcases. 'Help me, pl…ea…se.'

Rod stepped gingerly towards the voice. Pausing near the suitcases, he wondered for a moment what the Mexican bead-seller would do in this situation. But Rod was sure the bead-seller would have hijacked the tender, not become a helpless stowaway.

Rod walked to the source of the voice. Behind the cases it was in shadow, and for a moment Rod saw nothing. Then he did see.

He needn't have worried. The person who was lying on the ground, and groaning and crying in a most unpleasant way, was quite beyond doing harm to Rod, or to anyone else on this earth. It was a man who, Rod thought, might have been around forty. He was wearing very smart clothes and a jacket, as well as a bow tie. But this could not take your gaze off his eyes, which were small and mean, and reminded Rod of a beetle, or a small lizard he had seen when Beryl and Bernice's car had stopped. The man was sweating profusely, and all around him there was a most obnoxious smell of sweat and decay. Worst of all, there was a wide red wound just above the man's trouser belt, and his hands were feebly holding onto the wound while blood seeped all around them.

'I don't… have… much… longer,' said the man slowly, in obvious great pain and with a huge effort. 'Have to… tell… you… something.'

'What can I do, man?' Rod asked. He thought of making a gallant attempt to bandage up the wound.

'Nothing,' the dying man murmured. 'Nothing. Too late.'

Rod took off his camel-skin waistcoat and made a sort of pillow for the man's head.

'Listen…' gurgled the man. 'Listen… don't forget… don't… Tortoise… wanted… Tortoise was right. Much… too… dangerous. So ugly… Tortoise was right.'

Tortoise! Who was that?

'Who's Tortoise, man?' demanded Rod, but the dying man's words came from lips that were moving automatically, spurred on by a brain that had given up.

'Don't forget… don't forget this…' said the man, finally. Then he paused. Rod wondered if he was going to die, with whatever was so important left unsaid.

But it was clear that the man was only waiting to gather breath. He coughed, and blood was welling up now all over his hands from the groin injury. He coughed small spurts of blood too.

'What's your name, man?' Rod asked.

'My name's… Charles,' the man replied. 'Charles… Terrapin. Listen to me… Tortoise… the Russians in the Gloria hotel in Düsseldorf, West… Germany… laundry chute.' The man spluttered once more. 'Laundry chute,' he forced out again, and then that was it. More blood swam up from the wound in his groin, his face dissolved into a tightened grimace of agony and Charles Edward Terrapin, late grocer, late housebreaker, late husband, late assassin, prevented any further material becoming available to his biographers.

Rod watched in silence for a long time after the man had died. He had never seen anyone snuff out before. The peculiar smell of death lifted up from Charles's body and made Rod's head swim. Rod got up and looked about, hoping to find something to eat. What to do about the dead man was a problem, but Rod was sure it would be impossible to alert the drivers, whoever they were, before the vehicle stopped. He went towards the front of the moving tender, because that was as yet unexplored and because if there was a way of communicating with anybody in the cab, it would be there.

Moving along, on his left, he saw two things that stood out from the rubbish and old furniture that was everywhere. One of them was a large canister of gas, with a tube on top that led into a mass of sacking. The other thing was a great pile of white stuff in a hopper beside it. The white material was being very slowly funnelled away towards the top of the hopper, where it again disappeared behind sacking. Rod looked a little closer, and he saw that the white stuff was, in fact, bread, tiny pieces of chopped-up bread. But it was not very interesting, and any speculations Rod might have had about the apparatus were stopped by another noise that hit his ears, this time from just behind him.

He turned round, and his eyes met the eyes of the

best-looking girl, no, the most beautiful girl he had ever seen in his entire life. She had high cheekbones, very white teeth and light yellow-brown hair. She was slim and her tight white jacket was softly rounded by small, strong-looking breasts.

She was also holding a double-barrelled shotgun, and pointing it at Rod.

10

Not a beer

Rod stood still. No mucking about. Because even if this dab was the most beautiful one he had ever seen, she was pointing a pretty nasty-looking gun at him, and he was pretty certain that the man who had told him about 'Tortoise' hadn't died from natural causes. As Rod looked at the girl, who he thought was about twenty, two thoughts swept through his mind; one useful, that he had better be very careful, and the other crazy, that this girl was who he had been looking for in all the sweat, slozes and splicings of his life. But he said nothing.

Neither did the girl, for a much longer time than Rod would have imagined. Then she did say something, because she had opened her mouth and a noise had come out. But it was only a strange music, not words.

Rod put his arms up like cowboys did, then said, very slowly…

'Sorry, I can't understand.'

'You are a fool,' said the girl quickly in English. 'But I might have known that an Englishman could speak nothing but his own base tongue.'

Rod thought that this was rather harsh, but the two barrels like nostrils of an ancient ugly old woman, were also not friendly. So he said nothing.

'Who are you?' the girl said, lifting up the shotgun to Rod's face, her finger on the trigger. Rod felt that it was not the time for reciting his autobiography of the last five years, so all he said, keeping his arms firmly in the air, was – 'I'm a traveller.'

'A traveller?' she echoed.

'Yes,' said Rod.

The girl did not continue her interrogation. 'Sit down there,' she commanded, pointing with the gun to a pile of ragged carpets. 'I've killed one of you men already today. And I will kill another, if you do not do everything I say.'

Rod did what she said, and he tried to look as unaggressive and unmale as possible. The girl sat down about five feet from him, and kept the gun pointing at his face. Having reached some sort of rapport, and having grasped that the girl would not shoot him if he did as he was told, Rod looked at her without paying quite so much attention to the gun.

She was certainly exceedingly beautiful. Rod had not noticed at first just how beautiful she was, but now he looked at her much more carefully. Her ears, for example, were tucked inside her hair, but small parts of them showed and they looked like being the softest things for miles around. And although the girl had set her face in a hard stare at him, it was impossible for her to conceal a puckish sort of look that was imprinted all through her.

'Take your stupid eyes off my face,' ordered the girl, and so Rod looked at her legs, the upper parts of which were covered with a dark green and rather shabby skirt.

'Shut your eyes!' yelled the girl, 'Shut them, if you cannot look at me without betraying desire in your face.'

Rod shut them, and thought of the girl's voice. She spoke English very well, though in a careful, exact way. But her voice was wonderful, low and soft like a happy dream. Her accent, which pronounced all 'sh' sounds as straight 's', had a lisping charm, which gave Rod little surges of power between his shoulder blades. Suddenly, diving into his head, came the thought that he must stay alive. Stay alive to find out what was happening in the tender, why the other man had been killed. Stay alive to know the girl.

They sat where they were, looking at each other.

At last Rod said slowly, 'Well, dab - you want to know who I am?'

'You need not slow your speech,' answered the girl. 'I understand all you say. I speak fluent English. Do not think that because I am not of your kind I am of inferior intelligence.'

'My name's Rod,' said Rod, but still speaking slowly.

'I am not interested in your name. The other one told me his name and then I shot him. Beware.'

Rod did not move. The girl was studying his face.

'But I will not shoot you,' she went on, saying 'soot' for 'shoot'. 'Not yet. We have a long journey. I am bored. Before you die, you shall provide me with entertainment.'

'That's fine with me: I'm happy to provide you with entertainment for just as long as you want. Can I… well, can I ask where you're from?'

'You don't know? You can't guess? But of course not. What do the English know of people from outside their little island?'

'Well?' asked Rod, politely.

'I am Finnish,' said the girl. 'My name is Silja.' She pronounced it 'sil-ya',with the 'ya' like in the word 'yam'.

She kept the gun pointed straight at him.

'Sil-ya,' Rod repeated, but he said 'sil-dga' with the 'dg'

sounding like the 'dg' in 'badge'.

'No, no. In Finnish we pronounce the 'j' like the 'y' in English. Silja is a character in a story by a Finnish writer. You will not have heard of the story. But that is enough about me. You will explain why you are here.'

'I was chased,' said Rod, 'and this seemed the best place to hide.'

'Who chased you?'

'Some French throb.'

'Some *what?*'

Rod searched his mind to try and remember what *throb* was in the language of folk who didn't yawn the mud. Finally, he said: 'A French guy. He was a policeman.'

'Why was the policeman chasing you?'

'He thought I was a drug dealer.'

'And are you?'

'No,' said Rod.

'Are you telling the truth?'

'Yes,' said Rod.

'I see,' replied the girl. 'Did you see Terrapin die?'

'Yes.' Rod looked at the shotgun. 'He died… while I was watching him.'

'Did it hurt when he died?'

'I'm pretty sure it hurt *him*,' said Rod, 'and it wasn't much fun for me.'

'Good,' said the girl, and wrinkled her nose. 'I am glad he died a painful death. I did not like him.'

'Why did you shoot him?' asked Rod.

'Be quiet. I will ask the questions, I have the gun.'

That was certainly true. Rod had several other questions that he would have liked to ask. Like why there were no windows in the tender, what the gas canister and the bread were doing, where they were going. But Silja was doing the asking.

'I do not like you,' she said. 'I do not like any of you. Even as I sit here, I expect you are thinking sexual thoughts about me.'

To be honest, that very moment Rod was thinking of how he was going to escape. But as he had been thinking such thoughts all the other time that they were there, he didn't deny it.

'All men do nothing but think such things,' said Silja. 'My parents encourage them. My mother is jealous because I am beautiful.'

'Are your grunds... your parents driving this thing?' asked Rod.

Silja, who had been looking a little friendlier during this latest self-revelation, snarled and tightened her face full of hate. She stood over Rod with the gun.

'Shut up!' she screamed. 'My parents are nothing to you. Do not speak of them!'

At that point Rod did in fact think she was going to shoot him. The terrible vision of his own face blasted open and raw-red with hot pellets smashed into him for an instant. He snatched his arms to his head, but Silja backed away.

'See,' she said very slowly. 'How easy a man can be frightened.' Her voice acquired a dangerous, sly tone. 'You are nothing to me,' she drawled out. 'Remember that. If you talk about something I do not like, if you do not do exactly as I say, you will become like the one who is dead over there.'

Rod breathed heavily and was glad that his face was still intact.

'Now I am bored again,' said Silja, changing mood without

the least degree of self-consciousness. 'So to amuse myself I will ask you questions. You must answer them correctly.'

She did not mention specifically what the penalty would be for *not* answering them correctly. But Rod felt he could make a pretty good guess as to its nature.

'Where is Finland?' demanded Silja.

'Somewhere north? Somewhere north of Germany?'

'*Far* north.' Said Silja. 'Cold and in the north. Too cold for English fools to live there.'

'Sorry,' said Rod.

Silja paused.

'What does VALTA mean?' she asked, and Rod thought that there was a little smile on her face.

'I don't know,' said Rod.

'Of course not. You are a fool, as I said. It is a Finnish word. It means *power*.'

'Oh,' said Rod.

Silja waited, then she asked, slowly, again.

'What do you know about Urho Kekkonen?'

Urho Kekkonen was the president of Finland, worshipped and much loved by Finns at home and in exile. Adored even by those warped and made ugly by the past.

'Some sort of beer?' asked Rod.

Silja kept very still. Pointing the gun.

11

Winter

In the winter of 1939, almost forty years earlier, cold had become a habit. A great shackle of ice stretched across all Scandinavia. Trees hung for hundreds of thousands of square miles in an apparently lifeless pall of snow, their roots clogged and guttered by ice. But they were still growing. Skies shone an eerie blue, gleaming tufts of solid grey in the lands where the sun never shone. Horizons were bent to wispy unknown imaginings of frost, that swam out of view and swept miles beyond the eye. The glaciers and ice-held lakes that mark the confines of Finland were then taut in a ribbon of winter that seemed to have been there since the great mammoths had walked the earth, leaving their ponderous carcasses randomly embedded in ice for numberless winters to follow.

And, amidst this winter, the Russians had come.

At first the news came slowly. A hint in this village, a rumour among a few people in this town. The important men kept silent. They had known. And ice had gripped the land, making it fatal to go outside without a leather hat, or the warm shawl that the women wore.

The attack came, and crisis inflicted Finland once more. Independence, battled for in 1917 and won, had not protected the land. The frontiers were too wide, they could not all be protected. At that time, if life had any existence there, it was only to be found in the pockets of warmth in tiny, wood carved, and snow-swept houses that lay deposited in small clusters beside pine forests.

When the Russians had first come, VALTA was still young. Then, it was not even VALTA. Then, what would become VALTA were five young Finns, four strong young men and one girl who had lived, ignorant of the world beyond, in a Finnish village for twenty years.

Vilta, Aamu, Lahti, Taivi and Aino had grown up with the nature that surrounded them. In their cradles, the very words their mothers had taught them spoke a language of snow. The different kinds of snow, the creatures one might hope to find in it, the *peikot*, or trolls, that lived in the forests, some good, some eaters of children. What greater world did they then desire? When all was provided there, at the warm nipple of a loving mother, in the starlit gaze of a winter evening, in the folklore and culture of a thousand years. The five young children, then, knew nothing of the turbulences miles away, that would rob them of this world for ever. They had no ears for marching boots, rifles, tanks, massed rallies of hate, doctrines that wrapped their way around minds hungry for self-respect.

So the young people grew up, and as their characters grew stronger and more individual they would walk, sometimes alone, sometimes in groups, walking and now watching their mistress Nature on loftier feet, and with more conscious eyes.

'And that,' Lahti had said to Taivi, 'is the tenth bird with gleaming feathers that I have seen today.'

And Taivi had smiled, at the thought and at her.

For then, as they grew older, the men felt charged with

a secret power, a power that lay untapped in arms, legs, in minds, a power that spilled out into an appreciation of nature beyond even that which their own heritage could explain. And as the force of potential love coursed through their veins, nature seemed wiser, older, stronger, nature was charged with a potency beyond the mind of mere man. And Lahti, then fair-skinned, soft-voiced and finer than the undulating waves of wind-swept snow that piled about the village, received all the young men's best thoughts and dreams. Her body provided a mine from which they milked the yearnings of their own fancy.

And when the time came, they fought to win her, each in his own way. Vilta was a lover of the brooks, the myriads of tiny streams that picked their way among pine trees and clods of earth. There he would walk with Lahti, would coax her into remembering the names of brook-side plants, while she laughed to see a stickle-fish frightening intruders twice its size from its nest. Thus Vilta courted Lahti.

Aamu was quieter than he, and loved to cook quaint little Finnish dishes for his beloved, which he would gingerly produce for her amidst embarrassment and hopes, and which Lahti would eat in the light way of a girl, while her looks and body sent softly-voiced Aamu into a quiet, well-hidden ecstasy.

Aino was more vigorous, and had taken Lahti's hand one morning before she withdrew it from his grip and pointed to the chorus of blue lights that hung shimmering in the Northern dawn. He understood. How could he ever force love when the lights shone so mysteriously? Was it not better to acknowledge love's pain, and to bow one's head to the presence of love? Such things Lahti told to Aino that morning.

But Taivi received her. Perhaps his thoughts complemented

her own best of all, perhaps she saw in the harmonies of his body the wiser, romantic truth that her girl sense sought so keenly. The three other young men saw the reality, and dropped away. Fell back, to return to nature and to their own imaginings. To store their strength within themselves, until their own time came.

Taivi married Lahti, and loved her in every syllable her woman's voice produced, in every fold of her skirt, in every glance of her eyes, in every flash of her white woman's teeth. The Russians attacked, sweeping over Eastern Finland and Karelia in a Mongol horde. The four men fought. And Lahti, soaked with despair, volunteered to cook for the newly conscripted army. Perhaps, even in the trenches of war, she could resurrect nature.

It was a deathly hard, bitter struggle, but the end was never really in any doubt. As the vast Russian continent released thousands and thousands of eager, equipped soldiers, Finland lay trampled and exhausted beneath the cold, beneath the bombs.

Vilta, Aamu, Taivi and Aino, who had survived all attacks and a winter of starvation, were captured by the surge of Russians who finally spilled into the country, frustrated by the waiting and by the tenacity of a few thousand light-skinned snow rats, as they called the Finns. Lahti was also taken, and made to cook for her captors.

By this time the Russians thoroughly hated the Finns. They hated the cold, barren land in which they fought, they hated them for killing their comrades, they hated the low, strange, incomprehensible tones of the language they spoke. Now that so many Finns had been captured, there was the chance to send some of this malevolence to ground. Unexplained deaths occurred in the prison camps, reports of beatings, of blindings, of mind torture. But nothing was proven.

For Vilta, Aamu, Lahti, Taivi and Aino their time did not come until they had been prisoners for all the winter. In the prison camp by Lake Ladoga spring was battling through. Vilta heard the gurgling of thawing brooks on his exercise marches, Lahti felt life unwrapping from the desolate earth she trod. But already something had died within them all. No longer could they be innocent of the greater evil beyond the natural world of Finland and their early lives. They had all glimpsed something more terrible.

The end finally came for them when spring was sending shafts of thaw into the forests and by the lake-sides.

Though not death. That would have been far kinder.

When winter had finally gone past, the five Finns were reunited in a large camp fifty kilometres east of the town of Lappeenranta. Twice a day they all met for exercise marches, though Taivi and Lahti stayed well apart. It would not be good to show that they still loved each other. The war had taken its toll, and there was a dull seriousness in the Finns' faces that they all pretended was due to camp conditions. They knew that it was not so, and that the seriousness would now always be there.

One evening two guards came to the barracks where the four men were kept. Vilta, Aamu, Taivi and Aino were told to go outside. Lahti was already waiting for them.

The circumstances were only of limited interest. A Russian private, whose father had perished in the Winter War, had discovered that the five all came from the same village. None of the Finns ever found out his name, and what he was called is not important. But after the winter the guards were almost as hungry as the prisoners, and the Finns, with their natural placidity, could stand imprisonment better than the Russian overseers.

Vilta, Aamu, Lahti, Taivi and Aino met the Russian private in a small wood-walled room to which they were led. He laughed at them, and swore at them in Russian, though they did not understand. Still laughing, the Russian left the room, in a hurry.

As he ran out he threw a small PAK 3 grenade into the room. He was ten yards away when he heard it exploding from inside.

The grenade had the precise effect he intended. It did not kill, but it whirled round the room at a height of five feet, spraying molten aluminium in sticky, flaming bursts at the Finns.

They came out of the camp hospital about three months later, Lahti taking rather longer than the others. She had some mental trouble to deal with as well. By the time they came out the Russian private had been drafted elsewhere. The Russians were too busy with Nazi Germany to seek a criminal in their own ranks.

The war ended, and Lahti was first to return to the village. She had to explain very carefully who she was before they would believe her. But she remained loyal to Taivi, though now they were both so repulsive to look at that love was something that had vanished with their beauty and youth. Something else kept them together. It bonded them more when they had a daughter whom they called Silja. Silja was beautiful and Lahti saw that and died a little within.

So Vilta, Aamu, Lahti, Taivi and Aino died, and VALTA was born.

Banishing themselves from the land they loved, they went

to warmer temperatures in the south. They saw each other often, forming a patriotic group of five dedicated to taking revenge. Russians disappeared mysteriously in Marseilles at regular intervals for the next thirty years. For Vilta, Aamu and Aino the move was easy. Too ugly to stay, they lived lives bereft of company but each other. But once their lives had shrunken to mere dry vibrations on an old record, the pain was not so intense.

For Lahti and Taivi and Silja, the pain was worse. They suffered not merely a death, but a central pillar in their sanity collapsed to dust. The repercussions would take time, but meanwhile there were Russians to be killed.

In thirty years the three who had not won Lahti lived on, in some fashion or another. Aamu had his pictures of their earlier days, and he lived for seeing them each morning.

Lahti, Taivi and Silja planned. For they had suffered a kind of death many years ago, and what did they have to lose?

These are the events in the beginning.

12

Flashback

After terminating his brief acquaintanceship with Aamu and with Erasmus Scales, Charles had lain low for several days, literally, in a ditch near Aix-en-Provence. So low, in fact, that when he emerged at the end of the fourth day, his outer person was covered and spotted with large quantities of small crawling things. Spiders had draped their webs around his socks, and beetles were making love with great gusto in the pockets of his coat. The sun had risen and fallen four times, he had not eaten since before Aamu's meal, and his entire body was chilled and painful from the prickles at the bottom of the ditch.

But at least he was free, he thought.

Even if the two bodies had been discovered, Charles saw no reason why anyone should suspect him. He decided that it was time to go back, and finish the job Tortoise had, weirdly perhaps - but so much that had happened to Charles in his life seemed to him weird - entrusted him with. He'd decided that his period of hiding was over. There was, after all, the fifty thousand pounds to be earned.

Charles did a quick check of his unappetising person. All appeared to be present and correct. The Proconsul card was still there in his pocket, though rather the worse for its sojourn in the mud. Charles wiped it clean and nursed it back to creditworthy shape. As he went down the hill to Aix, he calculated that in only a few days all would be over. In England once more, eating well, drinking even better, women, money. The prospect was so wonderful he belched with excitement and walked faster.

It seemed to Terrapin amazing even now how one flash of the credit card, and his scrawled signature, brought people to his aid. Scruffy and unwashed, Charles visited shop after shop, always at first to be greeted by stares of hatred and repugnance. Ten minutes later, he walked out, the staff beaming like the Andromeda Nebula and Charles clutching yet another parcel. He spent the night in a luxury hotel, where he had a much-needed shower and after a dinner of fillet steak medium rare, tender new potatoes and fresh pea, he enjoyed a long sleep in sheets faintly scented with lavender.

The following morning Charles emerged from the hotel wearing a new suit. He ordered another beer from the waiter at a bar near the Old Port and stared speechlessly out of the window.

It had been a bad day for Lahti.

The throbbing in her mind, normally quiet enough to bear, had tortured her from waking when she had faced another day of death with her husband. All of Taivi's efforts, his embraces, his consoling words, had no effect. His scarred face, which Lahti could usually tolerate for at least the first hours of the day, now made the pains worse.

'And where is Silja? Where is she?'

'My love,' said Taivi from habit. 'She is gone to buy bread.'

'Is there not enough bread in the larder?'

'Bread. Real bread, rye bread,' Taivi urged her. 'Sit down, I will prepare food.'

Lahti sat down, drawing her shawl around her tighter. It framed her face of aged deformity. She buried her head in her hands. 'My pains, my God, my pains. Why will they not go? Each night I think... why are they still here? After so long?'

'I shall prepare food,' Taivi repeated, touching her hair and moving to the kitchen. 'Silja will return soon.'

'My daughter! She goes every day. Why can I not see her? I want to see her!'

'We must have someone to buy food, my love.'

'Why must it be my Silja? Why cannot you go? Always it is her. Why not you?'

Taivi did not answer. It was the pains. When Lahti was like this, he could only leave her. The pains would pass. Silja would return.

Lahti sat still, as her blood pumped furiously in her ears and the pains reached their morning height. She bent her head back, gave out a low whine and, in a torment of agony, opened and closed her eyes slowly, breathing heavily. The pains would go away a little if she did that. Her eyes took in the room, but did not register the image. It was a low room, stuffy with the smell of illness. With the kitchen next door and two tiny, even stuffier bedrooms, it made up the flat in which they lived, their home, since that night when they had fled south and made some sort of life there.

In the nearest bedroom Silja had been conceived, and in the furthest bedroom Silja now lived, surrounded by the smells of old age. In the largest room, the sitting room, were the same portraits and pictures of their earlier life that had been Aamu's only solace in his last days. Those images, and Silja, were among the only things that would make the pains go away. But this morning they were not enough, and Lahti's eyes flashed over the pictures of life and youth without noticing their joy. She breathed long drawn out breaths like those of a woman in labour, but only a noise by the door released the pain a little. Silja came in, and Lahti smiled inside. Outside her mouth was fixed in its harsh, cramped frown.

'Your mother, she is ill.' Taivi had come from the kitchen. 'Look to her.'

'Mother!' yelled Silja, seeing the old woman for the first time. And she ran towards her. Her touches and embrace gave the old woman strength once more, but Lahti would not show it.

'Away!' she cried. 'You come back late, and now you pretend affection when I am ill. With whom have you been walking this morning?'

Silja stood back and her mother looked her full in the face.

'With no one, Mother. Alone as always.'

'Yes?' challenged Lahti. 'Alone? I am to believe that?'

'Believe it or do not believe it, Mother,' said Silja, 'it is true.'

Lahti looked at her. After her early morning walk there was a pink flush in the girl's face. Her lustrous hair hung down by her cheeks. She was beautiful. Lahti said nothing.

Taivi came in with a bowl of stew.

'My love, let us eat. There is much to discuss.' He beckoned Silja to the table from where she waited, unsure, by the door.

When they were all seated, Taivi said, 'Now all three of us are completely alone.'

Lahti said nothing and Silja blinked a few times.

Taivi continued. 'That is why your morning walks must

continue to be lonely ones. We are in a weakened state. There must be no possibilities of enemies in our midst.'

Neither of the parents ever mentioned Silja's beauty as being a reason why her early morning walks were so risky. It was one of the things they never discussed.

Taivi sipped his stew, blowing on it to cool it. 'We are alone. Today I have read in the newspaper that our last friend is dead from a gun. I do not read who killed him. He is found with a fat Englishman who has been identified as one "Erasmus Scales". Perhaps our last friend was fighting him. But now our friend is dead.'

'All of them!' called Lahti suddenly. 'All dead?'

'Vilta, Aamu, Aino,' said Silja slowly. 'My uncles whom I loved.'

'Dead,' said Taivi. 'But we must gain strength from their deaths.'

He looked at Lahti who nodded slightly.

'You will listen, Silja,' said Taivi. 'You will listen very carefully. The agreement must not be thwarted. Not now.'

Lahti's pains were now a little better. Taivi gave a glance to the portraits hanging above him and said:

'A plan has been prepared for this event and it was arranged that the last ones would perform it.'

'Is that my concern, Father?' the girl asked, and rose to go.

'Stay,' Taivi stopped her with his hand. 'This time, yes. This time it is your concern. The last plan concerns the young as well as the old.'

He might have said the beautiful as well as the ugly, but he did not.

Silja returned to her seat and did not move.

'Listen carefully, my girl,' said Lahti. 'Do not think of the running boys on the beach but think of us.'

Taivi coughed and put both his hands on the table.

'When we all came to this warm city,' he began, 'we were alone, though there were five of us. Our beloved land was far away, and we had all agreed never to return. Because of the accident.'

Lahti looked at Silja's placid high cheek-boned face.

'And we stayed together until this year, when the uncles have begun to die,' went on Taivi. 'They all died suddenly. How is not important. At that time, we formed our group called Power, we decided that for the good of the world we would kill as many Russians as possible. That we have done, but in a smaller way than we expected. Now, at last, a chance has arisen to do more. And that is why we need your help, my child.'

'You are listening?' called Lahti to her daughter.

'Of course, of course, Mother. What can I do but listen?'

'It is dangerous,' said Taivi. 'There is danger for all of us. But for you, my child, there is the possibility of permanent Glory.'

'How?' demanded Silja.

'Be quiet,' called Lahti. 'Your father is still speaking. Listen to him.'

'My dear,' said Taivi, 'Silja is vital for our plan. This time we must talk well to her.'

Silja said nothing, but set her features in a stare, determined not to be upset by her mother's comments.

'In a few days' time a delegation of twelve Russian devils arrives at the Gloria Hotel in Düsseldorf, Western Germany. They are important people, and the German Republic hopes to make many advances from their visitation. We will prevent that. We will destroy them, and revenge ourselves at last for what we have suffered.'

'It shall be dangerous,' Lahti cut in. 'There will be many guards and enemies around the hotel.'

'And how are we to reach the Russians, Father?' asked Silja. 'We are weak.'

'Weak in numbers,' said Taivi quickly. 'Not in wisdom and daring. We are also strong and stubborn.'

'Have you a plan?' asked Silja, excited now.

'Yes, and you, my daughter, face the greatest danger of all. I obtained a map of the interior of the hotel some months ago. We can expect that guards will be positioned all around the Russian dogs. But there is a place underground, where the laundry is collected. We shall attack from there. I see no reason why there should be guards down there. After all, they do not know that we are coming. And you, my daughter, you will place the bomb that will kill them all.'

'Father,' said Silja, 'it sounds horribly dangerous.'

'I am afraid it is, my daughter. Indeed, it is likely that you will have to die to achieve the aim of our mission.'

Silja just stared at him. 'You are serious? I am to die?'

Taivi said nothing.

'How long have you been planning this?' the girl demanded. 'How long ago did you decide to kill me?'

'No!' cried Taivi. 'The purpose of the plan was never to kill you. Our only daughter, do you think we would do that if we did not have a reason? This way the objectives of our organisation, Power, will be completely satisfied. Even if we are arrested, we will know that we have gained revenge. We will not have lived in vain.'

'But what about me? How happy will I be, being dead?'

'A small sacrifice,' said Lahti. 'A glorious chance to die for our ideas. For our country. For Finland.'

'Besides, who can otherwise place the bomb?' Taivi demanded. 'Who else is thin and strong enough to climb the chute? Shall I do it? Shall your mother do it?'

They both glared at the girl, in whom the portraits above their heads sprang to life.

Silja was silent. But what could she do but obey? What other possibility could she have ever imagined? The thought of running away simply didn't occur to her. Perhaps if there had been someone in her life with whom she could have imagined having a new life, doing so might have occurred to her. But there wasn't and it didn't.

'The vehicle is ready,' said Taivi, taking advantage of his daughter's silence. 'We travel tomorrow.' He rose from his seat to prepare the midday meal. As he left the room, he turned back towards Lahti. 'Have we sufficient bread?' he asked.

Lahti said, 'Yes. Plenty for the journey.'

Taivi turned back to the kitchen quickly, as if his question had only been a mere afterthought.

13

Encounter

Lahti, Taivi and Silja, after a most melancholy day of arguments and rages, went to bed early. Silja remained awake a long time, naked on her bed. She clutched her knees, felt the warmth of her legs, and wondered what was going to happen. She was nearing sleep when she heard a rustle by her window. It was Charles, making an early start after a long night. Immediately Silja dived under her bed, as the window frame rattled, and was finally forced open.

A sinister-looking head peeped in through the darkness. Silja was under the bed and could see nothing, but she heard the scrape of metal against wood as the shotgun came in through the window. A scuttle, a nervous trembling noise and Charles was inside the room. He had come straight to the flat from his business engagement with the chambermaid.

Not a noise. Charles stood in the darkened room, by Silja's bed, and carefully took off his outdoor shoes. He knew that the two Finns were at home, as there was a light downstairs. Where they were, he did not know. But he would find them.

Hark.

Was that an owl hooting outside? Or a good demon of the night, protecting people from such intruders as these. Charles passed, shotgun pointing in front, and listened. There was a snoring noise coming from next door. People. Tortoise would be revenged at last. Though that was not the thought in Charles's brain. His thought was that at last the money was within his grasp. A battery of pleasant delights swept across his mind in a hurricane. He moved across the room to the door of Silja's room, and put his hand on the latch.

Under the bed, naked, Silja was so terrified she could hardly think. She caught her breath inside, and cursed her nakedness, that made her so vulnerable. Who was the intruder looking for? Herself? Her beloved parents? Beloved? At least, her parents were in danger. Her feelings ran high towards their protection, but she could do nothing. There was a click as the door opened and a gleam of light shot from the corridor into the girl's room. Charles did not look behind. There was a walk to the next bedroom, and then he would be there.

A three-metre walk to her mother and father's bedroom, Silja thought, and then the intruder would be there. Silja was naked, helpless.

Her parents intended to kill her, but she would protect them.

Immediately after the door had swung shut again Silja moved into action. She crawled from the bed and flung on a dressing-gown. All this with hardly a noise. She was so scared now that her brain was running on a different level, and in fact, inside, she felt quite calm. She gently prised open the door, as Charles flung back her parents' door and switched on the light.

The two sleeping Finns made some murmurings, half-waking at the disturbance.

Charles had prepared himself to hear a language that would make him feel queasy, but now that his target was so near, his brain was also working well. He pointed the shotgun at the two pillows. Maybe one would be enough. But he had put two cartridges in, just in case.

He had put two in. Or at least he thought he had.

Charles remembered as Silja appeared behind him.

Charles fired.

No blood, no guts, no screams of pain and grunts. Just a click. Tiny.

Click.

The other barrel. Maybe. Charles braced himself again.

Click. Very quietly.

There was no second chance.

Silja threw herself at Charles. She was not very strong and she bruised herself falling. He stood there. Enemies all around him. Just as before. GREEEEEAAAAAT. Kill them all. The swine.

Charles's blood surged through his body. So what if the gun wasn't loaded? It had two barrels. They would do. Raising his gun, he lifted it high and Taivi and Lahti were still hardly awake. But Silja was. She wrapped herself and her dressing-gown around his legs. Wrapped hard and low. With what strength she had left, she pushed hard and rolled towards him. Charles's swipe at the two sleeping Finns missed by half a metre. He crashed down on the carpet, but was still going to get up again when Silja picked up the gun and, using the wooden handle, hit him with it, very hard, on the back of his head.

Then she screamed, cried and cried, as Lahti woke up at last and yelled at her to demand what *that man* was doing, prostrate in their room.

14

A malevolent Finnish sprite

Charles had woken up this time in rather less congenial circumstances than those to which he had become accustomed since meeting Dr Tortoise. Instead of lying in a large luxurious bed, he was sitting in a wooden chair. It was clear that his current host had a genuinely hospitable nature, since Charles's arms and legs were so firmly tied to the chair that seeking alternative accommodation was quite unnecessary. There was a pain in his head that made the average hangover feel like a flea settling, and he was conscious that his clothes were in a certain state of disarray.

A completely naked young woman was sitting opposite him. A few feet to her left lay the shotgun, and Charles had a somewhat nasty feeling that it was no longer unloaded.

As he sat and watched, the girl stood up and performed a little dance. She lifted her hands slowly above her head, and twirled round and round, quietly and without quick movement. Then she moved closer to Charles and almost touched his face with her breasts, which were not like cranes but firm, softly rounded hillocks on her body. All natural and clean. From her serene, watching face, to the folded fair-coloured triangle where her body became forked, she shone.

He could not move an inch. Batting an eyelid was about the

limit of his brain's control over his body. No point struggling. He watched.

The girl lifted and lowered herself, her hair loose. She moved closer; then she moved away. Her bare feet ran over the floorboards of the moving vehicle like fluid.

Charles stared.

After about ten minutes (though only Silja was thinking about time) she drew to a slower pace and then to a stop. Charles was sitting in the chair, with the dignity and poise of an exhausted rat.

'You fool!' she yelled. 'You sit there helpless and you desire me. Is my body for you? With ropes about you? You who tried to kill us all?

'Hold on. Wait a minute,' said Charles. Subtler methods had to be tried. 'I didn't try to kill you. That's if you're their daughter. I only wanted to… talk to your mum and dad.'

'Talk!' cried the girl, and she ran towards Charles, sticking out her right index finger at him like a malevolent Finnish sprite. 'Talk! With a gun? Do you think I am a fool like you?'

'No, I think you're very beautiful,' said Charles. The girl was still naked and it seemed the right thing to say. But she sprang back at this with a shriek.

'So. You do think sexual thoughts about me! You do!'

Charles had decided it was time to move in for the kill. 'Come here,' he said, 'talk to your new friend Charles Terrapin. I only wanted to talk to your parents. There are some people who want to kill them. I know that. I had the gun because I wanted to offer myself to your parents as their guard.'

He waited to see what would happen. Still naked, Silja came close to him. She looked easier, more friendly. Charles carried on.

'Still, I can't blame you for getting the wrong idea. People often think people like me are out to do harm. Working for a charity brings these problems.'

The words ended on a stab of pain as Silja brought her fist down on his right cheek. She ran back to where the gun lay, and Charles hung his head again. A trickle of blood tasted bitter in his mouth before running down his chin.

'Listen, fool,' said Silja. 'I know all about you. You came here to kill us all. You see, I have this.'

She held up two things in the hand that wasn't holding the gun. One, Charles could see, was the Proconsul card. The other was the piece of paper with Tortoise's address on it.

'This man, Tortoise, is known to my parents,' said Silja, slowly. 'I never met him, but they told me about him last night. He sent you to kill us all. I expect it was you who killed uncle Aamu.'

Charles was in a dreadful state. He was in the grip of terror, combined with an overwhelming lust.

'My parents said I could do with you what I want. They gave you to me. So I thought, before I kill you, that I would give you a test. I hate all your kind, you men who think of nothing but sexual matters. You men are never satisfied. Your lust knows no limits. Never!'

Despair clogged Charles's soul. *Before I kill you*. So that was it. The money, the drink, the days of freedom vanished in a misty haze, and the nearest emotion Charles could produce to sorrow flooded through him.

'But I will tell you what we are doing. Just so you know how much you have failed. We are travelling north where we will plant a bomb in the Gloria Hotel, Düsseldorf, and kill all the Russians there. It will be our final triumph. I have been chosen to place the bomb at the top of the laundry chute. The laundry chute is very important. To ensure the success of our mission I shall sacrifice myself to make sure the bomb does what it is intended to do. So it will involve my death. But my parents have decided that. I will have a glorious death. Not like you.'

Silja paused.

'Tell me I am very beautiful,' she said. 'Say it in a nice, kind, soft voice, and I may still let you go free.'

But it was too late to ask for that. Charles had panicked. Niceness and softness were no longer qualities he could produce. In a desperate attempt to generate them, he blurted out *'you're very beautiful!'* in the forced scream of a cornered animal.

'Not good enough,' said Silja slowly. She put the gun to her shoulder and aimed at Charles's belly button. Perhaps a bit lower. Range of about five feet.

'No, no, no!' The words crawled out of Charles. 'Wait, please,' he finished feebly.

Silja fired.

Inside the gun, the hammer hit the cartridge, exploded the charge, uncrinkled the crinkled plastic at the front of the cartridge, and sprayed out the shot.

The crash deafened the girl for several minutes. A cloud of stinking smoke rose to the top of the tender and drifted into the air inside.

Silja looked at Charles. Her shot had landed in his groin, a little above the target. But it would do. She untied his ropes, kicked away the chair, and dragged the dying man to some sacking. She knew he would be dead soon. She was too busy to finish him off.

For despite her love for Lahti and Taivi, mutiny had begun.

Taking a piece of paper from her bag, she made an envelope with it. On the envelope she wrote:

TORTOISE
13 CATHEDRAL WALK
CANTERBURY
ENGLANTI

Silja forgot that the Finnish word for England would not quite do without a change in spelling. But the letter would get there. Then she took another piece of paper and slowly wrote on it, in the rounded handwriting of a girl. She hoped Tortoise did not know what Terrapin's handwriting looked like.

DEAR TORTOISE,
FINNS GOING TO GLORIA HOTEL, DÜSSELDORF. TO KILL RUSSIANS. I AM FOLLOWING THEM.
CHARLES TERRAPIN

But she did not mention the laundry chute.

When the tender next stopped at a service station for the night she told her parents that Terrapin was dying. By herself she posted the letter, using an express label and stamp.

The letter would take five days to get there.

15

Father and son

Back in England, Tortoise sat waiting for Charles. The old man had taken increasingly to his subterranean room since sending his assassin to work. Every evening, when his daily routine of business had ceased, he would come to his place below the cathedral, to think, to sit. For here, in the half-light and surrounded by the incandescent images of his son, he could be whole. He could shore up the past with these pictures and stop it ruining him. In his chair, his brown, aged, hard exterior lay, almost dead except for the fingers, which turned and revolved at the end of his arms in a permanent nervous anxiety.

But Tortoise was glad that Terrapin had not sent a message. That meant that things were going well. Now, these weeks after sending him after the Finns, Tortoise was certain Terrapin was going to succeed. One day Terrapin would return (Tortoise thought with affection of his employee's shabbiness and Terrapin's partiality for gin) and then all would be at peace. The past would finally be placated. Tortoise would wait for death without anger, without grief. And you, my son, would no longer cry.

The old man was ill. His breathing was slowly becoming more laboured, his movements slower and increasingly like the dead, inert way of a real tortoise. In every way the gnarled old man was waiting for death. Moving towards it.

But not yet. Not while Terrapin's mission was incomplete. Every day, in the bright mornings that Tortoise hated so much, the old man made the long walk to the bank in town. Just to check. Just to see that the job was being done. He received a statement from the cashier which told him how the European Express card was being used. There were massive expenditures for restaurants, for hotel bills, for wine merchants. Once, Tortoise noticed with great pleasure, for a shotgun. The money did not matter, as long as Charles was alive and doing the job. Tortoise had already opened an account for Charles at that bank, and the fifty thousand pounds was already in it. A crate of best London gin was waiting for the assassin's return in Tortoise's house.

Tortoise had lived the day a hundred times in his mind: the day when Charles would return, triumphant. The rather scruffy figure would come in, demand a drink and would probably not say anything until a couple of gins had vanished down his throat. Then he would say *I've done it*, or something like that. Nothing else. Tortoise would know that his revenge was finally complete. He hoped he himself would be able to hand over the bank account number, so Charles could get his money, without crying.

For he had cried so much, when it had happened.

Lahti and Taivi and the Finns had had their winter. Tortoise had had his. Twenty years earlier, Tortoise had not been an old man staring at pictures on his wall of his son. Then, Tortoise had been young, with his share of strength. His son had also been strong, in the very zenith of his youth.

Tortoise had been fifty-two years old in those days, his son twenty-one. They went everywhere together. As an internationally repected adviser on church restoration, Tortoise shuttled to the continent with all the regularity of a cross-Channel ferry. He and his son visited places that to most men were locations in films, Tortoise and his son went to them all, advising confused old theologians about their buildings, propping up the hopes of worried priests in tiny valleys. 'Your building can be saved,' Tortoise would say. 'I shall tell you how.' Tears of gratitude had so often accompanied his departure that Tortoise had usually said farewell with much the same words each time. 'Do not thank me. My son and I only wish to save your beautiful building. Thank only the God who inspired those who created it.'

At length, after success, fame and wealth had been their companions for many years, Tortoise and his son went to live in Marseilles. They had been given a villa by the sea. It was a gift from a priest whose twin-steepled church Tortoise had saved by advocating forcing concrete beneath the foundations in a special pattern that provided maximum supporting strength. The priest, who came from a family that had grown rich through owning a vast vineyard, left the villa to Tortoise in his will, and here they both came, to live in sun and clean air.

Tortoise's son read books, spoke seven languages and hoped to one day become an interpreter for the diplomatic service. At twenty-one there was no rush to do this, so he read and thought by the side of the Mediterranean. Always talking to his father, always discussing the most interesting questions of the day. And Tortoise, whose wife had died before their only child learned to talk, saw in his son the highest ideals and values. All the restoration and success only had meaning in that it meant he could be with his son. All the money only had a function in that it meant that they could live together in harmonious surroundings. And Tortoise's son, for whom his father had long been the only form of life that possessed intelligence and virtue great enough to interest him, read and talked. And hoped for the day when, as a wonderfully efficient interpreter in the places were the mainstream of men's businesses were conducted, he would himself have success and fame.

Tortoise had begun his career at about the same time as when the PAK 3 exploded in a room far north. He came to Marseilles when Vilta, Aamu, Lahti, Taivi and Aino had already lived there several years. But Silja was not, as yet, in existence.

Tortoise and his son got to know Taivi when they had met the disfigured Finn on an early morning walk. Tortoise could speak Finnish from spending several months in Helsinki years ago directing the restoration of the Uspenski Eastern Orthodox Cathedral there, and he and his son treated Taivi rather like a church that was in need of restoration. The friendless old Finn had even invited them to his flat. But Tortoise had not liked the Finn's wife and they did not repeat the visit as man and son.

Tortoise's son still met Taivi occasionally in a bar by the old port, where the young man practised his ability at one of the less common languages he was learning at that time. Eventually an invitation came to the villa from Taivi. The couple were having a large meal at Taivi's flat, to celebrate Finnish Independence Day. Tortoise declined. He was very busy at that time, preparing a dossier on certain renovations that needed to be made to Canterbury Cathedral. It was the greatest engagement of his career, and the one nearest his heart. 'But you must go,' said Tortoise to his son. 'We must not disappoint them.' Tortoise's son went.

They did not find the body for two months, when an old fisherman dredged up a headless, decomposed horror from the placid waters of the bay.

The police could not help. As far as they were concerned there had been a murder down an alley as the son was walking in the centre of the city. Such murders happened all the time. There were more important things to do than chase criminals they would never catch.

But Tortoise knew. His son had been a champion of Communist Russia. Always reading the politics, always studying the history. The son spoke Russian best of all his languages. Tortoise had not been concerned when, at their first meeting, Taivi had said that he and his wife hated the Russians. Tortoise had thought it would be a field for profitable discussion and opposition of ideas.

Tortoise went to see Taivi as soon as the first wave of his grief had passed. He was met with derision, with hatred. What did they know of the son's death? He had been killed on the way there that night, hadn't the police said that? Tortoise stayed in the flat long enough to find his son's Finnish-English dictionary, which the young man had taken, just in case, on the night of the meal. He held it up at Taivi in a burst of despair. But Taivi had taken it from him and put it in the fire, then he sent Tortoise away.

Tortoise returned to England. He had been given a house by Canterbury Cathedral, with one special feature, in thankfulness for his work on the great building. He was becoming old, and his grief was so great that for many years he did nothing but make the house the correct place to nurse his grief. Then he advertised, and in due time Charles arrived. Then sitting, sitting, staring at pictures, for a lifetime.

And now this. With the post that morning.

> DEAR TORTOISE,
>
> FINNS GOING TO GLORIA HOTEL, DÜSSELDORF. TO KILL RUSSIANS. I AM FOLLOWING THEM.
>
> CHARLES TERRAPIN

A little research in the daily newspapers and Tortoise knew just who the Russians were in the Gloria Hotel. So this was it. VALTA was making the biggest effort of all.

And this time, yes, he would act. Though his breathing was getting more difficult, though he was now probably, unfortunately, dying, he would act. Maybe Terrapin would get there before he did. But Tortoise wanted to be among those around when they caught Lahti and Taivi. When they caught them for the last time. Until now, his age and frailty had always put thoughts of avenging his son's death *himself* out of mind. But this was the big one. This was different.

Tortoise booked a flight to Düsseldorf, leaving in two days' time. That would be enough to set his affairs in order.

He also left a letter with his solicitors addressed to the chief constable of Canterbury police. They had instructions to send it twenty-four hours after Tortoise's flight left London.

The old man was well respected in Canterbury. The police would take notice of what he said.

So, now he waited. Sitting, in the half-lit room, staring at the hundreds of faces on the wall. Always staring, immersed in the past, in his grief, staring and remembering.

But this time, at last, with the chance of action.

16

Naked

Silja started to strip in front of Rod. 'I was foolish,' she said. 'I was much, much too good to you. But now I am wise.'

She took off her shirt with remarkable dexterity, considering she was pointing the gun at Rod all the time.

'I thought you were better than the other one,' she continued. 'I thought you deserved a chance to survive, but you do not.'

Off with the sleeves, only a tight black bra beneath.

'Now! We will see whether you are really better than him.'

Rod watched, as she put her bra by her side. Her rather large, firm breasts were held taut by her muscles. Rod said nothing. It was clear Silja did not like him saying anything. After the discussion about Finland, which Rod went through with considerable ignorance and considerable unintended rudeness, Rod started asking her questions about where they were going. And every time he said 'are we going south? Aren't we going south, dab? To the south of France?' she raised the gun and laughed, looked as if she was going to shoot him. Though she did not.

And now this. 'Why do you know nothing of my homeland?' demanded Silja. 'My country is beautiful. The snow, the lakes that lie so still, the pine trees. My people are beautiful, lovely.

Clean and fresh, like the snow and the brooks.'

She slowed here, speaking as if from memory. Talking as if somebody had made her learn it. Rod still said nothing. He still had no idea where he was going, or what was happening. It only mattered now to stay alive, and to try and see what was on the bean with this dab. Shutting up was best. The dab went on and on, in English, fortunately, so at least he could understand what she was on about.

'And our language. Our speech. It is so wonderful, like listening to the songs of birds in the early morning. It rises and it falls, like a lark above a field.'

There was a great deal more of the same kind of thing. As Rod switched his mind off from the slozing nonsense Silja was saying, he tried so hard to think of how to get out of it. But it was no go. Rod was pretty good at guessing how fast a car he was in was going, and the tender was not exactly travelling at a speed where you rushed to leap out. In any case, there was not a window in the place, just the same soft light as before. The back door, he was certain, was locked, and the floor was solid metal. Plus the fact that there was a girl a few feet from him, pointing a gun, and a girl who had already killed once.

But what a place to die. What a slum! The stink from Charles's festering body had filled the tender. The smell churned high and hot by the sun outside. All around, filthy old stinking sacking and carpets.

And in front of him, now with no clothes on, this dab. Clean and sexy as hell. With a gun, and threatening.

'I see,' said Silja, quicker now, 'that you are not listening. You think my speech too uninteresting for you, perhaps. We shall consider that. And I will tell you why I have removed my clothes.'

It was something worth explaining, thought Rod. Yes.

'All my life,' said Silja, 'men have thought sexual thoughts about me. They are always the same. They are never satisfied. Never!'

Rod looked her full in the face. Any lower and it would have been tricky.

'The one I shot,' said Silja, 'The one called Terrapin, was also thinking sexual thoughts about me. I shot him because of that, and also because he tried to kill us.'

Terrapin! So that was the poor throb's name. He had not forgotten what the dying throb said. *Tortoise was right. Tortoise was right*. Then, *the laundry chute*. Yes, Terrapin had mentioned that. And then the name of a hotel: the Gloria hotel in Düsseldorf, West Germany

Charles and Tortoise. Code names, maybe? Rod wondered.

'So now it is your turn,' said Silja. 'I am now with no clothes at all. Do you not think that I am beautiful? Do you not think I am beautiful here... and here?' With the other hand and without a trace of pride, she indicated the two main areas of her to where Charles's eyes had been inclined to wander. 'Well, do you not think I'm pretty?'

She looked at Rod, and he looked at her.

'If you do not think sexual thoughts about me,' said Silja, 'we will talk a little. If you do...' She sighed a little. But not much.

There was a familiar stirring between Rod's legs. Immediately he felt that, he saw that Silja had fixed her large, gorgeous eyes down there. She was looking. A thought rammed home. Of course? She raised the gun, and Rod felt the stirring grow. Oh no. Grooooowing. And bigger.

Silja put the gun to her shoulder.

Sloz!

She was going to shoot. DOWN THERE!

Well this is it, Coaster. No more slozes, no more silence in country lanes, no more scraping the tar, no more yawning the mud. Flashing past him, all his slozes, walks, thinking, chats, hopes, everything. Was it all about to be gone?

The Mexican bead-seller. What would he do? Think. And quickly.

Wise, that throb was wise and bright and got the best of every situation, every slozing time. So THINK.

Easy.

Rod shut his eyes.

His hardness began to fade, his thoughts cooled down, his eyes were closed. And Silja took the gun down, towards the floor.

Rod didn't see it. He waited.

No noise.

Then she spoke, as if she were tired, worn out. 'I had not thought you could do that. That was clever.'

Rod thought it was pretty bloody obvious, but he didn't say that to Silja.

'So… you're not going to kill me, dab?'

'No. Not at the moment. I shall put my clothes back on.'

There was some rustling sound.

Rod opened his eyes cautiously. A minute or so later, Silja was dressed again.

'Anyway,' said Silja, as if what had just happened had not just happened, 'Now that I know you are clever, I am not bored. We still have a long way to go.'

It seemed possible, now, to ask a few things.

'Dab… I want…'

'You may now call me Silja,' said the girl. 'I have said that that is my name.'

'Dab… Silja. I mean, like, where are we going? I'd just like to know, in case you're going to kill me.'

Silja actually laughed.

'You are still frightened. But there is no need. Perhaps later. But now we can talk.'

'Are we still going south? South of France?'

'No,' said Silja.

'Where, then?'

'To Germany. We are travelling to Germany. Why did you think France?'

'Because, dab, it's…' *Germany.*

'What the hell for?' cried Rod, without thinking.

'Do not shout at me!' and the gun was back at him. 'You may ask questions. But do not shout!'

'Why West Germany?'

'I must not tell you,' said Silja. 'My parents would not like it.'

'I was going south, to the south of France,' said Rod. 'I want some rest, dab, I'm going to a commune.'

'What is a commune?'

'A place, a camp, where throbs and dabs go to rest it.'

Silja looked at him with her beautiful puckish face at a slight sideways angle.

'Why do you not speak properly? Did you not learn your language well when you were younger?'

'I guess I'm scared,' said Rod. 'The words just happened.'

'Explain to me what is a *dab* and a *throb*,' said Silja. Only she didn't say *throb* but sort of *frob*. That was her accent. 'Explain that to me, and I can understand you a little amount.'

'It means a girl and a guy; a man,' said Rod, feeling strange using the orthodox words. 'Only there's some folk that live in houses and some that scrape the tar. If you scrape the tar you say that.'

'Again,' cried Silja. 'Scrape the tar? What does that mean?'

'Travelling,' said Rod. 'Living on the road.'

'Oh,' said Silja. 'Well I will try and remember.' She was silent for a moment, then said: 'You have passed my test. I will not kill you yet. But am I not beautiful?'

'Yes,' said Rod.

'Good. Now I know. And you will not talk about me in that way again.'

'OK,' said Rod. This was better than he expected. Having prepared himself to snuff out twice already that morning (if *it was* morning) this was slozing good. But still so much to ask. Rod decided to try and make a bit of headway. If it didn't work he could always shut his mouth, or his eyes.

'So it's your grunds… your mum and dad in the cab then?'

'Yes, I suppose you must have guessed that. My mother and father are in the cab. My mother is driving.'

'So why are you here?' said Rod. 'Why aren't you with them?'

The girl's answer was quick and firm.

'I was told to remain here. So here I am.'

'And they don't know what you're doing, dab?'

'No,' said Silja. 'They cannot hear anything from the back here. There is no window.' She drew a sigh and said, '*Perhaps* they heard the noise when I shot the other one.'

'And they'd have heard if you'd shot me?'

'Perhaps. But as long as I remain here, I am allowed to do what I wish to do.'

Rod cleared his throat. It felt good still to be alive. 'Tell me about your grunds,' he said, quietly. 'Your parents, I mean. Your mother… is she beautiful?'

Rather strangely, Silja placed the gun on the floor, with her hand off the trigger. She got up and walked away a little. Then she turned around, and looked Rod hard in the face. He was pretty sure that if he dived now, he could get to the gun before Silja did. The curious thing was, he found that he didn't want to do that.

'No, and she is jealous of my undamaged face,' said Silja. She had started to breathe more heavily and a more normal expression had swum over her face.

'Undamaged?'

'That is what I said, yes.'

Rod decided not to press Silja for any more details.

'Why? Is she not like you, dab?' *Tread carefully here, very carefully*, he thought. So what if he managed to grab the gun? He still had to get out of the tender. And those grunds in the front had a gun, most likely. Maybe one each. Maybe more.

'No, she is ugly,' Silja spoke quietly, slowly. 'Her face is burnt. Her cheeks are not soft. They are burnt. They look like the cheeks of a tortoise. Cold and burnt like that.'

'And your dad?'

'He is the same. But he is a man and for him it is not so bad. They are all like that. Burnt.'

'Were they born like that?'

'No. There was a terrible event. It happened a long time ago, before I was born. A Russian man did it.'

She sighed again, closed her eyes, and sniffed. Crying? A bit, yes. 'It was so bad… so long ago. My poor mother, my poor father! And I am so beautiful. They are not.'

Another sore point. Rod had never met a dab so slozed up. He did not move from sitting on the floor, but pushed things a little more.

'They? Who's they? More of them? More in the family?'

'My uncles. They are all now dead. All dead except my parents. And my mother is jealous because I am beautiful.'

'So she's jealous. Who cares? Scrape the tar, clear off. Run away.'

'No!' Silja shouted, but stayed where she was. 'What would they be without me? I am their daughter. Where would they be without me? They need me. They love me.'

'That's why they shut you back here?' Rod called.

'They need me,' Silja said. 'I am important… important for them. For the plan.'

'The plan. What plan?'

And Silja sat down and cried and now she was by herself, alone, without a gun and Rod could have grabbed the gun if he'd wanted to and made her *his* prisoner. He didn't. Silja started to cry, and then she whispered to Rod. 'The plan. Why we are going to Germany. Why I am here.'

'They need you? What for?'

'I am going to have to die to make the plan work,' Silja said.

Rod just stared at her. 'Are you serious?'

'Yes.'

Silja started to cry again.

Rod and Silja were now sitting on a pile of sacking near the back of the tender. They were about five feet apart, but Rod did not want to touch her. It was not the place to splice anyone, not with the stink in the tender and Charles's body fifteen feet or so away on the left. Not only that, but as Silja had talked (as she had done for about the last half hour) something peculiar had happened to Rod.

It was like this. Once, while hanging about Portobello Road, on one of the Sundays when the Mexican bead-seller was no longer there, Rod had picked up a pottery egg about six inches long. It was one of those things that you could split in half and then find another egg, slightly smaller, inside. He did it again, and again and again, until Rod had laid seven eggs along the counter. Though he didn't buy them.

That was what it felt like now. At first, talking to Silja, he wanted to splice her. But now, with all the things she'd said, he didn't want to. Right now, Silja was like the egg.

Too much going on inside to splice her. Too many parts, you picked up one egg and there were all the little bits inside. So poor Rod, stuck looking at the eggs. And poor Silja, stuck with her eggs.

'Dab, I'm not going to let them kill you. You're not snuffing out. You got that?'

'You can do nothing. My parents want me to die and I must die. It is the plan. And the plan is more important than me.'

'That's a load of crud,' said Rod, but nothing else. When Silja had told him that she wanted to die, for the plan, Rod thought the dab had been kidding. Now he knew she hadn't been. Now that he knew the plan, Rod could see why the grunds had put the dab in the tender, so she wouldn't get into any trouble. She was important.

Change the subject for a while, Rod thought. He went to the part of the tender where he'd seen the bread and the canister.

'What's this for?' he called to Silja.

She came up to him, still five feet away, her head slightly sideways as she sometimes carried it.

'That,' said the girl. 'That is nothing. Only a gas… that is it… oxygen. And that by the side is food if we run out. Bread. My parents told me all about it.'

'Oh,' said Rod, and didn't press it. 'I get it dab, oxygen and food.'

He helped Silja hide Charles's dead body under some tarpaulin sheets. The place began to smell a bit better. They talked about a few more things, and Rod learned the Finnish for *please* and *thank you*. They were getting on pretty well, Rod thought. Meanwhile he tried to think of a plan.

He didn't tell Silja the one thing that had been worrying him ever since she told him about the bread.

If it was a food store, why had the pile of bread in the hop shrunk to about half the size it had been?

The tender, with Silja's parents in the lorry cab at the front, rocked to the side of the road and stopped. Rod grabbed the shotgun from the floor and told Silja to hide behind a pile of sacks.

'No,' she said. 'Please,' and she held out her hand for the gun.

Something in her face, and he hadn't even spliced her.

'OK,' said Rod. 'OK.' He found that, somehow, he somehow had no choice but to give her the gun. And he did give her the weapon, with its wooden handle and long evil-looking barrels.

Lahti saw Silja before she saw Rod, and exchanged a few words in their lark-like language. *Is the other one dead? Yes,*

Mother, very dead. Then Lahti saw Rod.

'Hi,' said Rod and smiled. Sloz, she was ugly! But much too old to be blowing people up. Silja had been kidding, surely.

Lahti gave a harsh cry. Silja stiffened.

'Dab,' called Rod. 'At least make her put her hands up!'

But Silja didn't do that. Instead she turned the barrels towards Rod.

Lahti said, in English, 'You will come with us.'

Very original, grund, thought Rod.

But the barrels were on him and he knew there was still a cartridge inside and Rod knew he had survived twice and he didn't want to die now. Back to the start.

'I'm sorry, Rod,' Silja said. Then, louder, 'Please, hurry up!'

17

Nasal affection

A lushly furnished, efficiently decorated room in the depths of the London Gloria Hotel, principal hotel of the famous chain that dots Europe with places of rest, relaxation and quiet. A noisy, restless hotel, with porters scurrying about, guests hurrying along in their relaxing visits, waiters dipping their fingers into remnants of massively expensive meals and later feasting off the leftovers. Sprawling and overpriced, the London Gloria led the way for the twelve other hotels in the illustrious Gloria Hotels chain.

And in this room, He sat. In this comfortable, carpeted room, with reproductions of Old Masters on the walls, including Vixen's favourite painting of all time, *The Flaying of Marsyas*, He dwelt. This carpet, this innocent Axminster, received every day the pacing prints of His feet! The drinks cabinet, sentinel of alcoholism, gave forth daily its benedictions unto His lips! And the telephone, once (so long ago) a mere item on a production line, transmitted His voice!

Now it transmitted that very voice, for He was at his desk, making a telephone call. At the switchboard outside the incoming calls to Him were, as usual, mostly all blocked, though now and again his secretary answered one at random to say, *He is unavailable. Perhaps some other time...*

Always the sentence unfinished. For who should expect to contact Him? One might as well try to telephone God himself. Though the creator had doubtless more lines, and was less often engaged.

Now, the electrons were singing joyfully through the wire. The diaphragm was proudly vibrating on the speaker. Such electronic bliss, to carry His tones, even on such a short journey from His room to the switchboard! The electrons died in their millions as the call was made. But what greater fate, to perish in so noble a cause?

'Hello, Miss Fallopian. Can you please bleep Vixen? I wish to see her.'

'Yes, sir, of course, sir, now I'll do it right away at this moment,' replied His secretary.

'Thank you,' and He replaced the receiver.

To return to His work, the daily check of all employers and guests seen through the (concealed) close circuit televisions that lined the kitchens, halls, reception rooms, and everywhere. An accurate, up-to-date dossier on them all. Their movements, their actions, what items they had picked up and which ones they had put down. Any discrepancy meant they were trying to steal from the Gloria hotel chain, which was the ultimate crime. Laser lights viewing guests as they went out the hotel service (or guest) entrance. To make sure.

Thirty years on the police force before retiring with the rank of chief superintendent and joining the Gloria hotel chain had left Him with no allowance for error. Simple logic. Check everybody, and any malefactors will be found. For who, which man, woman or child, which boss or washer-up, was free from the potential taint of crime? Silently, intently, purposefully, deliberately, He surveyed the cameras, and filled out the report. Long nose, tall, balding head, small moustache, slim, trimmed and docketed, Chief Superintendent Pickling Fox-Foetus went about his activities. On his door it said in golden letters (that yet gave so little indication of the hive of force within!) CHIEF SUPERINTENDENT P. FOX-FOETUS. COMMANDER OF SECURITY. Of the entire glorious Gloria hotel chain, Gloria Hotels International.

'And are there no richer guests this evening?'

'Sorry ma'am, it would seem not.'

'No titles, no higher salaries?'

'Only Mr Loaded, ma'am, and he's leaving tomorrow.'

'Then listen,' and the woman who spoke turned her tiny red eyes at the chief receptionists. 'This isn't good enough. Do you think I expect to come here to visit you and find this? I expect guests here, not the riff-raff from off the streets. And if *you* cannot acquire them, we will find someone who can.'

'I do my best, ma'am,' said the chief receptionist, almost in tears. She was a very young girl, and seven months pregnant.

'Your best is not enough, is it? This will cease forthwith.'

Her rebuke also ceased forthwith as two more guests, an elderly married couple, came trotting happily through the big swing doors towards the reception area. At the Gloria Hotel London, spies from the office found out the annual salary of every guest who had booked. It was forbidden, on pain of a visit from Miss Eustachia Vixen, to have a booking list with too many salaries below the prescribed average.

Miss Vixen now left the young girl and turned to the new arrivals.

'Your names?' she blurted out, as soon as they were close by.

A very feeble-looking man, in a voice that appeared to come from his chin, replied: 'Common. Mr and Mrs Common. We booked.'

Immediately Vixen's eyes swerved down to the booking list. There was a very small figure for Mr Common's monthly income, and it was listed as wages, not a salary.

'Indeed?' said Vixen. 'This is the London Gloria Hotel. Have you made a mistake?'

The two Commons paused, and then Mrs Common who was, if anything, even meeker and weaker-looking than her husband, said, 'Oh no. This Is the hotel, definitely. I mean I know this is the right hotel. We checked with our travel agency before leaving Birmingham.'

'You did?' Vixen said, nothing else. She surveyed the pair as if two large pieces of elephant dung had just that moment fallen from the ceiling to where they stood. She then gazed significantly at the chief receptionist, who was trying to hide in the corner, not very successfully.

Vixen stared back at the couple and then she asked:

'Was it horse racing or the football pools?'

Mr Common looked at Mrs Common and Mrs Common looked at Mr Common.

'Sorry?' said Mr Common, in a hamster-like voice.

'Or perhaps a rich relative died suddenly?' said Vixen.

The couple made no noise, except for possibly Mrs Common, since there was a tiny, bubbly sound coming from *somewhere*. Though it may have been the central heating.

'Large redundancy payment?' demanded Vixen, pressing home her advantage.

Eventually, after another pause, Mr Common said:

'We think we resent the inference... what you say. That...'

'Resent?' asked Vixen. 'My dear sir, there is no need to *resent* anything. I am merely curious to know how a man in your position can afford to spend time at this hotel.'

Mr Common was rapidly making a timid approach to anger. His wife said, 'It's my last week alive,' in a quiet voice.

'I see,' said Vixen in a very quick, rough manner. 'and of course you want to spend it here, do you?'

'My wife's dying and has a week left,' said Mr Common. 'So I sold all our furniture just to give my wife a nice week before she dies. We've never been in a hotel before. We've booked a room on the seventh floor. My darling wife shall have a nice view of London for the last week of her life.'

Vixen marched around the counter to the front. With her long, ape-like arms she took the Commons' luggage from them and deposited it outside. She then grabbed them both by their skinny shoulders and pushed them through the revolving doors, shouting at the porter not to allow them back in.

'Really!' Vixen yelled, red with rage. Mr and Mrs Common were scuttling timidly away outside, like frightened mice. 'These lower classes!' Vixen exclaimed. 'I never cease to be amazed at their impertinence. The lies they'll tell to get a week's free lodging at our hotel! A week left, indeed! A week at our expense, more like, then a moonlight flit!'

'But it says in the diary for next Monday that room 713 will need an undertaker that day,' replied the head receptionist, timidly.

'And I suppose you are going to tell me that these riff-raff would have been in that room?' cried Vixen.

'Yes, ma'am.'

'Nonsense! All part of the trick.' She moved more closely to the head receptionist, grabbed the girl's necktie very firmly, almost throttling her, and said:

'Your job is to help obtain respectable customers for this hotel, not down and outs. Carry out your duties properly and you may be allowed to stay. Otherwise I will report you to Chief Superintendent Fox-Foetus.'

The girl, who had managed to wriggle out of Vixen's grasp while the sylph was talking, opened her mouth wide with horror. 'Oh no, ma'am, please, not Chief Superintendent Fox-Foetus! *Please don't mention this to him.* Think of the poor innocent baby I'm carrying, ma'am.'

Vixen stared contemptuously at the girl's belly. 'Baby! I'll give you *baby*, that you can mention such a thing and Chief Superintendent Fox-Foetus in the same breath! It is enough to warrant your instant dismissal.'

'Please don't dismiss me, ma'am,' the girl pleaded. 'My husband lost his work last week, and I don't know how we'll manage as it is.'

'You will be judged according to your performance,' said Vixen. 'Not according to the whims of your renegade mate..., husband.'

She said this last word with a loud sniff, curling up what was left of her nose into utter contempt. The girl was crying freely now.

Vixen left. After this mild admonishment the girl would no doubt improve for a few weeks, and then they could sack her in the calm knowledge that Gloria Hotels International had extracted the very last piece of good work from her.

Vixen's bleeper bleeped. She found a telephone and called His office.

'The chief superintendent would like to see you, ma'am,' said Miss Fallopian. Vixen smiled an obnoxious crooked smile as soon as she recognised the voice of His secretary. So, she was summoned. Who knew what bliss lay in store. She was required, in His room!

Thirty seconds later Vixen was inside the chief superintendent's sacred chamber. At the desk sat Fox-Foetus himself. As he began to pour Vixen a sherry, she reflected how badly earthly titles summed people up. For just as all forms of life earning less than £10,000 a year were fuel for her general hatred, the chief superintendent, with his efficiency, his ability, his knowledge, and above all his big long pointed nose, was for her the only object on the third planet worth beholding with respect, apart from herself.

'Thank you, Pickly, thank you,' said Vixen, happy in her intimacy with Him, which enabled her to use the affectionate form of His name. 'Has anything particular arisen?'

'Indeed,' produced Fox-Foetus, from his lipless mouth. 'A matter of grave consequence. I was compelled to speak to you personally.'

What an honour! Vixen's face appeared to begin low down on her short, plump, pear-like body, turned red with excitement. How his nose shone so finely when he made an announcement of this kind!

'Tell me, Pickly, inform me.'

'The news is most disturbing.' Fox-Foetus leaned back in his chair, as he had done in the days when questioning a helpless suspect in the Force. His back was straight as a concrete block, and his moustache and nose bristled with utter power. 'Today I have completed the usual check of all our employees and all our guests. The dossier is completed, but one entry is unsatisfactory.'

Such glorious efficiency, such a power of nose!

'Who, Pickly? Who is the culprit? Tell me, your doting assistant, and I shall perform the required duty.'

Fox-Foetus's lipless voice issued out in a dark, sonorous tone. 'It is employee number 387/c/p,' he said. 'But I shall also make you acquainted with his name. that I have been watching him for some weeks now.'

'So his crime was anticipated,' said Vixen quickly, for Fox-Foetus never watched anybody who did not sin eventually. The chief superintendent slightly inclined his nose, in appreciation for this recognition of his powers.

'It is Pawn,' said the chief superintendent.

Vixen had no idea who Pawn was, but immediately Fox-Foetus had said the name she burst in with: 'Him! Of course, Pickly, I had also expected that the lower-class person would come to no good. But I never presume before you.'

Another nasal inclination from the great man.

'What has the miscreant done?' demanded Vixen, her voice charged with respect and admiration.

Fox-Foetus paused. He placed his hands on the desk. On the opposite wall, the wallpaper lay in its stuck situation, waiting for the chief superintendent to make his pronouncement. Distant in the solar system, the asteroids paused too, in their orbits, and aliens dozens of light-years away stopped eating with their long, sinister tentacles and waited, too.

'Miss Vixen, I am a man of quiet passions. My greater moods are devoted to my work. But in a case like this, I, too, can feel anger.'

Passionate man! thought Vixen.

'387/c/p,' He went on, 'the one they call Pawn, who washes up, who works in the kitchen, whose mother is ill, who is not rich, who…' said Fox-Foetus. At each of these successive clauses, Vixen, charged with reverence and general adoring emotions, leaned a little further forward in her chair. At the last 'who' she fell onto the floor.

Fox-Foetus watched her with his nose as she got up.

'Over-enthusiasm, Miss Vixen,' said the chief superintendent.

'It must be so,' she said. 'but you speak… you talk…' She stopped. Her emotional fibres tried feverishly to produce something like affection, but the effort was too great for her.

'I was speaking,' said Fox-Foetus, 'of our friend Pawn. Who has access to food storage rooms.'

'You mean…' postulated Vixen.

'Yes,' said Fox-Foetus.

'A great deal?' demanded Vixen, with wondering eyes.

'Sufficient for our purposes. *More* than sufficient.'

'Tell me the worst,' said Vixen, baring herself to him like Prometheus on his rock.

'You wish to know?'

'I *must* know,' produced Vixen in a plaintive wail of compulsion.'

'Then I shall tell you,' said Fox-Foetus. 'Miss Vixen, action must be taken. The concealed cameras provide indisputable evidence that 387/c/b, the one they call Pawn, has stolen a rasher of bacon.'

18

Pawn

Inasmuch as Vixen was capable of any emotion, it needs to be said that, despite everything, she did not love Fox-Foetus for his efficiency, or for his unavailability. True, he liked to believe that these were the reasons for her passion. But they were not.

In fact, Vixen's love was due to purely nasal causes. Just as nature had bestowed upon her a short, squat body and red, pig-like eyes, it had left her with a nose not much larger than the average pimple. This gave her face a most terrifying aspect. Contrariwise, Fox-Foetus had as his main feature, a nose as long as it was persistent. It stuck out, indeed, like a peninsula.

Vixen loved it. She loved its length and its tapering width, she loved the way it moved about, roughly in time to Fox-Foetus's face. She loved the way in which it prodded forward as Fox-Foetus nodded his head. Together as a nasal average, they had a good-sized nose each; as it was the discrepancy in noses allowed the mystic element of passion to enter. So much the better for Fox-Foetus and Vixen. So much the worse for 387/c/p, the one they called Pawn.

The following morning, Fox-Foetus and his adoring assistant took the personnel lift to the service floor. It was not yet seven o'clock, and birds were chirping their joy outside and millions of alarm clocks all over the land singing out their detested chimes. Fox-Foetus and Vixen heard nothing of this.

So little did they know of life outside the Gloria that news of an impending atomic attack would have taken at least a day to reach them in the depths of the hotel. The hotel ran itself so smoothly, in such an all-inclusive, disgusting sort of way, that life Outside was not regarded as relevant. The doors slid open, and a solid wall of kitchen air met the security duo's lungs, though Fox-Foetus inhaled far more than his assistant.

'Rather strong this morning, Vixen,' he commented, as they strode to where 387/c/p would be found.

'It's these lower-class workers, Pickly. They never wash.' As Vixen marched along, her arms swinging low down, face tight with devotion and dislike of everyone else around her apart from Fox-Foetus, Vixen constantly looked from side to side. It was a habit, a relic of the time when no cameras surveyed the hotel. Now, every square inch was constantly monitored and recorded on a video disc, which Fox-Foetus would play back later in the day to check activities. Now, Vixen performed her surveillance action to let the workers know their place, as well as to impress Fox-Foetus.

And certainly there was much to see that morning. With customers upstairs slowly beginning to wake up and yell for breakfast into their telephones, there was activity everywhere. Metal stoves shone heat onto the streaming cooks' faces, and the aromas of eggs, bacon, toast, milk cornflakes, fruit, belches, beans, swam around everyone and clung to walls. Clinking trolleys passed by with plates piled high and sweating boys pushing them. Great clouds of steam lifted high from coffee and tea-making machines. Pressurised hot water hissed constantly.

Curses, shouts, and abuse rang round the vast kitchen as finished food was jammed into the service lift, accompanied by a little docket and the imprint of the sweaty forefinger of whoever had last touched the food.

None of this Fox-Foetus and Vixen noticed, for they were too taken up with the purpose of their mission to have any thoughts for breakfasts, or for the comfort of guests. Such things were of no importance. All that mattered to them, now, was to catch the Culprit. They reached the end of the kitchen, where the great steaming demon, the dishwashing machine sat. It perpetually devoured and disgorged enormous rows of plates and pots. The washers-up surrounded the machine, jumping in and out of its blasts of steam as they grabbed plates to be dried. Fox-Foetus went up to the Chief Cleaning Supervisor (who was in charge of the washing-up machine) and they had a few brief words in the CCS's office. *Of course, sir, Assistant Menial Pawn was working. Yes, they could see him at that moment.* The CCS sniffed. He hoped it was nothing serious.

All the washers-up, and indeed all the hotel workers with the marginally less creative jobs, wore overalls with the letters AM (assistant medial) and then their numbers, sown onto the top pocket. Their names were not worn. Wearing names only encouraged 'friendships' among workers and as Vixen was always quick to point out, friendships among the lower workers were only detrimental to the working of the hotel.

It never ceases to amaze me, Pickly, how these lower workers preserve the capacity to form friendships of the emotional kind with each other. Thus Vixen pondered to herself while *Pickly* was with the CCS. She hoped to use the sentence to her great chief at some appropriate point.

'Are you in truth 387/c/b?' demanded Fox-Foetus. 'Is your name… outside… Pawn?'

No answer.

Vixen whispered in the chief superintendent's ear. 'I saw his lips move, Pickly… He said *something*. But he's too damned low to raise his voice.'

'Will you speak up, sir!' said Fox-Foetus. This time Pawn shouted as loud as he could. Vixen thought she heard a kind of mewing sound, but Fox-Foetus still heard nothing.

'387/c/b,' began the chief superintendent, but fortunately at that moment the CCS came out and said that if it was Pawn they were wanting to talk to, the little fool had lost his speech the month before after getting terrified when he saw Vixen for the first time, and if they gave Pawn a piece of paper he could answer. Paper and pen were found, and then Pawn wrote down his answer in block capitals: *YES, MY MOTHER DOES CALL ME PAWN.*

'And you, sir,' said Fox-Foetus, 'have been seen stealing a rasher of bacon. The evidence is overwhelming. Will you confess?'

At that moment all of the chief superintendent's body, but particularly his protuberance, bore down on the washer-up like a satellite's laser beam.

Pawn went even redder (as far as that was possible) and hung his head even lower than it was positioned in normal life.

'So, sir, you admit the crime?'

There was another pause. The other washers-up had now ceased feeding plates into the demon and also stopped to watch Fox-Foetus and the victim. After a great deal of shuffling about and redness, Pawn, who had been carefully avoiding looking at Vixen, timidly took up the pen once again. He wrote: *I TOOK IT FOR MY MOTHER*, whereupon Fox-Foetus triumphantly snatched the confession away from him. Shaking with fear, Pawn now wrote on another piece of paper: *SHE'S NOT VERY WELL AND IT WAS HER 90TH BIRTHDAY AND I WANTED TO GIVE HER A TREAT.*

Vixen snatched this paper from Pawn and read it. Pawn screwed his eyes tight shut to avoid having to look at the fair enslaver, who, with a scornful laugh ripped the paper into little shreds and threw them onto the floor.

'Anything of importance, Miss Vixen?' asked Fox-Foetus.

'Not to *you*, Pickly,' said the red-eyed heroine.

His supremacy once again affirmed, Fox-Foetus turned round to the gaping washers-up, '...will you return to your duties, please!'

The creepy duo, with Pawn firmly sandwiched between their nasally complimentary bodies, strode away.

The CCS watched them go. For the rest of the day he had a curious, inescapable feeling that Fox-Foetus's stare had included *him*, amongst the workers who had to return to their duties.

Dr Tortoise's plane had taken off after unexpected delays. When he was still frailly flying over the Channel, his solicitors opened the letter. Ten minutes later they were onto the police headquarters. And ten minutes after that, Chief Inspector Geddem had heard about it.

'None of our blinking business,' Geddem had said to the sergeant in charge. 'So Tortoise thinks there'll be some sort of trouble over in Germany. Is that my problem, then?'

But he ordered the sergeant to make two calls. One was

to New Scotland Yard, who would relay the information to Düsseldorf police. They would check it out.

The other call was to the Gloria Hotel in London.

'It is Fox-Foetus's firm, after all,' said Geddem. 'I ought to let him know.'

Then he laughed and told the sergeant that he and Fox-Foetus had once worked together for about five years.

'Hard-working chap, he was,' said Geddem. 'Astute fellow. Brave, too. Doesn't care much about his own safety. But he was always taking up with diabolical women. Maybe they find his big nose a turn-on.'

The sergeant could not get through to his office, but being able to mention an old friend, he persuaded Miss Fallopian to let him have a line to the great man as soon as possible.

'And so, Pawn, you have confessed. Is there anything else you wish to say?'

It was Vixen who spoke. Her body trembled with the shock of Pawn's crime. Her nose struggled for greater expansion. By her side stood Fox-Foetus, stern and lipless. In front sat the entire kitchen staff of the London Gloria. They were in the canteen, where all culprits ended their employment at the hotel, with Vixen and the chief superintendent ramming home the awfulness of the crime. The sixty or seventy onlookers felt some of Pawn's shame. Who knew who might next stand where he stood? Who could foresee whom the random hand of CRIME might next touch?

Pawn was silent. A close observer might have seen the tears that trickled like flowing gossamer down his cheeks.

'This man... this Menial,' and Vixen paused in her

deliverance. The onlookers thought she ceased to provide further effect in her attack on Pawn, but in reality it was because she had noticed how beautifully Pickly's nose shone where the electric light caught it.

'This man has been proved a culprit. The only possible penalty is expulsion. But first we wish you all to see him for yourselves. In order that you may all improve. In order that you may all avoid his Fate.'

Sighs from the spectators. More tears from Pawn.

'But wait,' said Vixen, raising her arm like Neptune stretching his trident. 'This culprit is no mere criminal. He has also put forward a reason, an excuse for his crime.'

Yells of '*Tell us*' and '*Shame*' depending on the attitude the gathered Menials had towards Pawn.

'Well?' cried Vixen, prodding Pawn as if he were a turnip being tested for freshness. 'Explain. Tell them what you told me.'

Silence. No one dared speak. What reason could there be for the theft?

MY MOTHER, wrote Pawn. Vixen read it.

'Your mother!' cried Vixen, in a voice that made the foundations creak. 'Your mother! What can she have to do with this business?'

SHE'S DYING OF CANCER!

'Dying! And well she might, with a son such as you!'

But Pawn had written a continuation. *AND SHE LIKES A BIT OF BACON AT HOME. AND I CAN'T AFFORD IT, NOT WITH MY WAGES.*

Vixen was speechless with rage. She was also speechless with love for her superior, who had stood through all this like a saint, as the traffic of human judgment was enacted before him. But now was the time to intervene.

'Beware, all of you,' said Fox-Foetus slowly. 'That you never suffer his fate.' He now addressed the whole of his nose to the former washer-up. 'Pawn, we are not interested in your mother and her no doubt numerous diseases. The facts of the case are undisputed. You have stolen a rasher of bacon. There is only one possible punishment.'

With his nose still horizontal he undid the front buttons of Pawn's uniform. So suddenly, Pawn was naked (apart from his shirt and trousers). No longer a Menial. Now a mere man of the street. He burst out crying, all the tears visible now. But the mood of the onlookers was against him. They could imagine receiving his fate themselves, and any show of sympathy would have singled them out for suspicion in the eyes of Fox-Foetus. Vixen gazed reverently at him. Such eyes he had! No criminal safe within his range of vision.

Pawn walked, in full flood of tears, out of the back door, which led directly from the canteen to the harsh world outside. Bereft of Gloria Hotel protection, to sink or swim in the morass of walking people.

Fox-Foetus ordered the onlookers back to work. When they were alone, he told Vixen to burn Pawn's uniform, and to scatter the ashes over the dishwashing machine. It was the most wry touch the Chief Security Officer had allowed himself in many years.

As Vixen's horrible body sweated and vibrated in approaching orgasm, her cries became more ecstatic. 'Pickly,' she yelled, biting hard on his nose. Her mind dissolved in depths of passion, and she muttered hysterically to herself, 'Oh nose… nose… nose,' with the said article firmly clenched between her teeth.

'Are the monthly reports ready?' asked Fox-Foetus through his mouth, although it didn't sound much like that. Though he was naked, he preserved his unavailability and efficiency by discussing business at such moments. It was always a rather one-sided conversation.

'If they are not,' said the chief superintendent, 'I would be grateful to have them at my desk by tomorrow week.'

This last word was particularly appropriate, as Vixen had by now finished and was semi-conscious on the sofa, totally weak. She had bitten marks into Fox-Foetus's nose, but she had not succeeded in actually biting the protuberance off. Her moments of greatest fantasy involved that very action.

The telephone rang in the office.

'Strange,' thought Fox-Foetus, rolling off. He had given orders that even fewer callers were to be allowed through than was usual.

'It's very important, sir,' said Miss Fallopian. 'And as it was from your old friend DS Geddem, who is apparently now a chief inspector, I thought you would want to speak to him.'

'Thank you, Miss Fallopian,' said Fox-Foetus. 'Please, put him on.'

The next five minutes he spent saying, 'Yes' and 'I see' and 'yes' and 'possibly', while Vixen recovered her viciousness once more. When she was once more dressed and adoring he spoke to her with unusual haste.

'Miss Vixen. Please attend carefully. Our branch in Germany, the Düsseldorf Gloria, is under the apparently imminent threat of a terrorist attack.'

He drew his head back and looked down at Vixen. She thought that she had never seen his nose so magnificent.

'Miss Vixen,' said Fox-Foetus. 'Activities here must be temporarily suspended. Our duty lies elsewhere.'

Vixen stood up. 'I am ready, Pickly,' she said.

'Return to your office and pack. I will book a flight at once.'

Vixen went towards the door, her heart was full of love and nasal affection.

'Oh, and Miss Vixen…' began Fox-Foetus.

She turned back. What words would he now bless her with? How could he match her own love, when her heart was overflowing? What might such a great, efficient, important man say to his woman, his lover, his adorer?

'Next time please bite a little further back,' said Fox-Foetus casually. 'It makes it so difficult to sneeze.'

19

Tug of love

It was amazing, crazy, slozing ridiculous, but, hell, it was happening. They had taken Rod to a room in a German motorway service station motel on the Autobahn about eighty kilometres south of Düsseldorf, and now this.

'*What has he said to you, child?*' Lahti asked.

Silja was honest, always honest to her parents. '*That he does not want me to die.*'

'*He does not want! What can he want? What right has he to want anything?*'

All of this Rod heard as he sat in the chair. Understanding nothing. The old grund, whom he took to be Silja's father, was standing near, with the shotgun. The two women were babbling away in that weird lingo Finnish, and Rod hoped Silja was saying nice things about him.

But, sloz, her grunds were ugly! The two faces of the old ones in the room made Silja's beauty stand out like something miraculous. And still Rod sat in his chair wondering why the girl, that lovely girl, was paying so much attention to the old crone by her side.

The crone was now saying something to the old throb. Of course Rod couldn't understand a word.

'*We must teach Silja that young men are evil,*' said Lahti. '*We must teach her that now. Who knows how she may betray us, if she will continue listening to such young men. And the end of the plan so near!*

They kept a guard on Rod for the next day. Either one of the parents, or Silja, took it in turns to watch over him with the gun, while the others slept or ate.

Whether it was Taivi, Lahti or Silja, when they were alone they said nothing to Rod, only pointed the gun. Rod did what he was told, because just before the guard had begun Lahti had said, using Silja, who spoke now, to interpret.

'We do not care about your life,' Silja said, blankly, translating her mother's Finnish. 'But if you do all we say, we may keep you alive.'

Now after a night (at least) had gone by, Rod was there, tired and hungry, and all the Finns had returned.

'*You, my girl, will interpret,*' said Lahti. Silja nodded.

Lahti moved nearer. Her horrible face was now only a few inches from Rod's face. He could see her teeth, ragged and with long roots, and he saw the exposed blood vessels beating in her cheeks. Silja was by her side, that girl was with her. And Silja's face was now as hard and staring as her mother's. All of the puckisness was quite gone.

During all that followed, the old woman barked something out and looked hard at Rod, while Silja repeated it in a voice almost as vicious to Rod.

'We know,' called out Silja. 'We know how it is that you men think. All through the life of my daughter we have been careful, watching that young men do not trap her. We know how it is you think.'

'An accident, dab. I got there by accident. D'you think I

wanted to get mixed up in this lot?'

'Your desires are quite evident. My daughter has already killed one of your kind. It is clear that you said love-talk to her!'

Lahti looked hard at Silja, and then Silja repeated, slowly: 'My daughter is a girl easily affected by love. She cannot control her baser emotions.'

'Dab,' called out Rod, who had slowly realised that the two old grunds could not speak English much. 'Dab. Sil, why you doing this? Your grunds have flipped out, dab.'

'Say nothing to me,' barked out Silja. She was holding the gun again. 'Do not pretend to me. I know how you men think.' She pointed to Lahti's face. 'See? This was done by a man's anger.'

Rod yelled out. 'Was that my fault? Was it? I don't know anything about it, do I?'

'You,' yelled Lahti, now in English. 'You were not even born at that time.'

'So?' said Rod, suppressing his surprise at hearing Lahti speak English, 'how can you blame me then?'

'It does not matter. You are a man. You are a young man. That means it's your fault.'

Lahti paused, and stood looking at Rod, breathing hard.

She spoke. Silja caught it.

'So we are going to make sure that you do not like my daughter any more. From this day, you will only hate her.'

How? thought Rod. *How were they going to do that?*

'We will show you how little my daughter is moved by you. She listens only to my commands. Therefore, you are of no importance.'

With Silja looking on, Lahti suddenly proceeded to remove

all Rod's clothes apart from his underpants.

It was most upsetting, being naked apart from his underpants in front of Silja and her mad grunds. Rod wanted to cry for help, to chase the grunds away, and to run away with Silja somewhere.

'See,' said Lahti. 'See how foolish you are, and you would take my daughter away, would you? The conceit of you men. When all the time you are like this, without clothes and helpless.'

'You made one big mistake, Coaster,' Silja said to him, in English, a few moments later. 'You forgot that my love for my parents is far greater than my love for any man could be.'

She stood there, and pointed to them.

Rod didn't say anything. Was this really Silja talking as herself or because her parents wanted her to say these things? It was impossible to be sure. The puckishness was even more absent from her face, yes, but wasn't there *something* in her eye?

'See,' and Silja spoke, 'What your love has done to you. See how foolish is your desire to help me. I do not wish for your help. I wish only to obey my parents. And now, just so you know how much you have failed,' said Silja, 'we are now all going another eight hundred kilometres towards Finland. To the north. We shall visit the Gloria Hotel in Düsseldorf and there we will take our final revenge. And I will receive the chance to give my life for my uncles and for my parents. I am proud to die for them.'

Silja fell silent for a moment, then said:

'And so no longer trust to love,' said Silja. 'Love will humiliate you, as you are now made into a fool. And love will betray you and make you weak. Those who love always become fools.

They will always become as you, full of pain and suffering… We have lived our lives without love, and we are real people. Not fools. Not idiots, running after things they cannot have.'

Rod just stood there and listened to all this. He wondered if Silja was going to shoot him dead at any moment.

20

The Daily Squalor

Rippoff Airways Flight 313 from London to Düsseldorf left Heathrow at six minutes past eleven exactly, and was scheduled to arrive at one thirty-five in the afternoon, local time. In the business class compartment, next to each other and sleeping, reclined Fox-Foetus and his admiring lover, Vixen. They had packed in an enormous hurry and were using the one and a half hour flight time to rest until their arrival.

A hostess flitted by, carrying a tray full of drinks, all of which had been laced with sleeping tablet fluid to make the passengers as untroublesome as possible during the flight. Her fairy-like tread, however, woke the chief superintendent up. He shook his head, sniffed twice, then used his left forefinger to check that his nose was still in position.

'Oh, waitress,' called Fox-Foetus.

The hostess turned and suppressed her manic anger at being addressed like that.

'Have you a copy of *The Daily Squalor* I could have a glance at?' asked the chief superintendent. 'Could do with catching up a little on the world news.'

'Of course, sir,' said the hostess, making the *sir* as ironic as her desire to keep her job allowed. But Fox-Foetus was still too dreamy to notice.

She returned a few seconds later with a copy of the beloved newspaper. Fox-Foetus yawned as he skimmed through it, only folding back the pages when he reached the crime section. He settled his nose and prepared to read.

Next to him, still ensconced in the deep mists of Lethe, sat his charming lover. Sleeping, her little red eyes were screwed up tight, her great arms wrapped around her chest like a nightmarish Egyptian mummy. Fox-Foetus noticed with a certain pleasure how her nose became alternately scarlet and white as the blood ebbed and flowed through it. He returned to reading his paper. Vixen looked far too blissful for him to risk disturbing her, and in any case there was a most interesting article in *The Daily Squalor* advocating bringing back the death penalty for shoplifting. Fox-Foetus read it with professional keenness and his nose twitched back and forth as he pondered on the possibility for eradicating crime that the article's proposal indicated.

A little further on (about two hundred miles, to be precise), the small-nosed nymph began to awaken. She gave an indication of this by making a few hideous snorting noises, and then producing a quantity of snot through her delicately featured nasal orifice. She shook herself like a water rat that had just emerged from a dank canal, wiped her nose with her left sleeve, and presently another pair of eyes was staring down at the article.

'Ah, Pickly! I dreamt about you! We were together on an island, with complete control of all the natives. You see, you and I were the only ones with guns, and so they all had to obey us! How fine you were as you issued your commands!'

'An important part of controlling one's subconscious, fantasies,' said her long-nosed chief after a few moments. 'It augurs well for your future mental health, Vixen.'

'I had never thought of that,' she said. 'But you are correct, as ever. I wish I had your ability to remember such technical details, Pickly.'

'It will come,' said Fox-Foetus after a short pause for self-congratulation, 'with time. Meanwhile, please read this article, I may wish to discuss it with you on future occasions, and it is as well that you are familiar with its contents.'

Vixen scanned the article, her eyes working like laser beams.

'Damn good idea, Pickly,' she said, presently. 'That would make the wretches think twice, wouldn't it?'

Fox-Foetus laughed and smiled a little, as if to indicate that his mate had caught his thoughts exactly.

'Of course,' he said. 'We should not neglect the fact that many people, particularly women, I believe, steal from shops to prevent their children from starving, but...'

'Hang 'em twice,' said Vixen. 'Too many children in the world as it is.'

Fox-Foetus smiled once more. Really, Vixen was making considerable progress, for someone who only six months ago had been a ticket collector on the London Underground. She was becoming the perfect echo of his own (though naturally more profound and creative) thoughts.

The happy pair thumbed through the rest of *The Daily Squalor* together, Vixen's horny thumbs sometimes touching the chief superintendent's slim, delicately manicured fingers.

The paper's first section contained extensive and detailed coverage of UK and global news, and occupied pages one and two. *The Daily Squalor* paid particular attention to trade union disputes and to the supposedly unreasonable behaviour of working-class people. A typical *Squalor* headline would be: BLOODY YOBBOES WANT 10% MORE, or THREE LESS TO WORRY ABOUT, the latter headline concerning itself with the deaths of three millworkers in Yorkshire who had gone on hunger strike to be paid their wages. The next section of the august journal, from pages three to ten, dealt exclusively with the Royal Family, and carefully explained what the Queen was wearing that day, also describing in details the Royal corgis' breakfast.

Then there were six pages giving readers advice about personal problems; advice furnished by agony aunt Lady Angela Japonica-Madeira, which was in fact a pen-name of Jeff Hackington, the editor of *The Daily Squalor*. Jeff wrote almost all the letters 'sent' to Angela and took care to ensure that about eighty percent of them focused on sex.

A typical Jeff letter was 'from' a nubile young housewife somewhere in the Home Counties, happily married, who finds herself falling in love with a similarly nubile and happily married lady friend and asks for advice: *I've never been to bed with a woman before, but I just can't stop thinking how wonderful it would be to make love with Susan. Please help me, Angela! Love from Kate.* Angela invariably recommended that the reader followed her impulses: 'You only live once, after all' was a frequent parting piece of advice Jeff provided.

The next section, which was the one that interested the nasally complementary couple particularly, contained features about such things as cruelty, and punishment. Then there were about a dozen pages of sports news and finally a prize crossword puzzle containing clues such as 'Definite article, three letters', 'Not thin, three letters' and 'Opposite of boy, four letters'.

'*Ladies and gentlemen, we shall shortly be landing at Düsseldorf Airport,*' said the captain's voice, '*Will you please secure your safety belts.*'

The plane swooped low and circled the airport twice to lose height. Fox-Foetus and Vixen were firmly entrenched in their seats. They swallowed several times as the plane's altitude reduced. Vixen only lost her terrified look when they were zooming along the runway, the wheels screeching as the pilot applied full brakes. Finally the plane arrived at Düsseldorf airport, West Germany, and the hostess reappeared.

'Would business-class passengers please step this way,' she said, and the pair unfastened their belts and followed her. In fact there were no other business-class passengers on the plane. This had somewhat upset Vixen, who had anticipated asking Fox-Foetus, in a loud voice, questions about the prestige of his position as Chief Security Officer for the whole Gloria Hotel international chain.

Once through customs control, the two charming lovers strode violently through the long, shining, glass-covered alleyway. All around them were tearful people hugging long-lost friends, exchanging presents in delighted excitement and reuniting in an ecstasy of happiness. None of which Fox-Foetus and Vixen noticed, Vixen merely adding, 'emotional friendships, Pickly, we know what that leads to,' in her most sinister tone possible. Fox-Foetus nodded, sagely.

They left the airport and Fox-Foetus hailed a taxi outside. In the fluent German he had learned from watching old films of Nazi rallies, he told the lower-class German person driving the taxi to take them to the Düsseldorf Gloria Hotel.

The Düsseldorf Gloria was the latest addition to the continent-spanning Gloria Hotels International chain and was set in three acres of lush waste ground. The main features of its surroundings were an old air raid shelter and a large quantity of extremely prickly nettles. All this, naturally, tended to be seen more by the workers than the guests. The employees, who all wore the usual Gloria uniforms with a personal number sewn on, filed like the Pied Piper's rats into a gloomy little service entrance, covered in soot and dried blood. On the other side of the building the guests were welcomed by a great canopy that stretched for fifty metres from the foyer, the walls of which were carefully designed to obscure the debris and rubbish in the hotel's grounds.

The building itself stretched up into the sky like an enormous grey thumb.

'What a marvellous place!' exclaimed Vixen in uncontrollable delight as the taxi drove towards the canopy. 'When I see places like this, Pickly, I realise that the lower orders will not have the final victory.'

Her eyes surveyed the concrete heights of the hotel like a proud admiral inspecting his favourite ship, and her face took on an expression that was the nearest she could manage to a smile.

'I am of your sentiments exactly, Vixen,' said Fox-Foetus. 'It only remains to be seen how effective the security arrangements are in the building, and for us to make sure the Russians are properly guarded as soon as possible.'

The hotel manager welcomed them at the entrance. He introduced himself as Herr Gewalt, pronouncing the 'w' as a 'v', and, it turned out, all his w-sounds that way too. He had a small moustache and brylcreemed, combed black hair with some strands hanging over his forehead, and an Austrian accent. He summoned a Turkish gentleman, whom he referred to as *Schweinhund*, to take the luggage into their room. The Turk touched his forehead, bowed, and ran up the stairs with the cases.

Fox-Foetus watched him go with an approving expression on his face.

'I see,' he said, 'that you do not allow the hotel porters to use the lifts. That is an idea that our hotel in London does not yet employ.'

'Indeed not,' said Gewalt. 'The lifts are only for the use of guests and higher employees.'

He glanced round in a somewhat guilty fashion.

'Vich effectively only includes me and my assistant Herr Donner. Ve consider it best for the foreign vorkers, the *Gastarbeiter*, you know…' here Gewalt paused and spat on the floor… 'to obtain physical fitness by using the stairs.'

Gewalt handed the duo their key. 'As you can see,' he said, 'Our little friend from Turkey has only had to climb to the ninth floor this time. He has been lucky. Please make yourselves comfortable in your room, at half past one vill you please join me for lunch, then ve vill discuss all security arrangements.'

The room was one of the best in the hotel, which meant that it had two televisions and also a clean lavatory. Fox-Foetus and Vixen went in, almost falling over their cases, but pleased to see a bottle of champagne lying in an ice-bucket on the dressing-table. There was a little handwritten note around the neck of the bottle, which said:

I VISH OUR FRIENDS FROM ENGLAND VITH

THIS BOTTLE VELCOME, and then a name, *HERR BLÖDERSAUFER, Beverages Manager.*

'Excellent, Vixen,' said Fox-Foetus. 'We must be indebted to our German friends for providing what I will venture to call the most appropriate present possible for our visit.'

He sat on the bed, his nose beginning to twitch with approaching sexual desire.

'An hour to ourselves would not be too great a self-indulgence, would it, Miss Vixen?'

'Oh, Pickly!' cried Vixen, in a passion of nasal love and admiration. She leapt upon him. But Fox-Foetus said, 'a moment, Miss Vixen,' and she waited until they had both drunk all the champagne amidst a mass of gurgles and snorts.

'Very well,' said Fox-Foetus, his nose now trembling so violently that it really looked as though it might tremble itself off completely.

Vixen, whose ape-like arms were so long she could touch the floor with her hands while standing up without having to bend down, tore the clothes off her squat, obnoxious body, then pulled the chief superintendent's shirt over his face, taking care not to damage his beloved nose in her haste. Fox-Foetus carefully removed his efficiently pressed trousers. Vixen rolled onto her back, her arms and legs sticking out like growths on a potato. Fox-Foetus knelt above her, Vixen pulled his head down and *ah the bliss* as her pig-like teeth dug into the organ on which all her most profound fantasies were centred.

At half past one exactly, Gewalt knocked on the door of room 913. He knocked again. Fox-Foetus heard it and untwisted his limbs from where they had been pressing the fair sylph to the sheets.

'A moment please,' called Fox-Foetus as he opened a couple of windows. He slapped Vixen's face a few times to bring her out of her sexual coma, and then they both dressed as quickly as possible, under the circumstances.

Fox-Foetus opened the door.

'I did not vish to disturb you,' said Gewalt apologetically, 'but lunch is served and it vould be unvise to postpone reviewing security measures for too long a period of time.'

'Of course, of course, I understand,' said Fox-Foetus, who, now that his clothes were on, was once again the utterly efficient great man. Vixen followed him out of the door, and the three marched off down the corridor.

Gewalt wiped his brow, and kept his breathing nice and regular. It would not be good to give them any hint that he had watched the past hour's entertainment through the keyhole.

21

The worm turns

Gewalt took Fox-Foetus and Vixen for lunch in one of the hotel restaurants, where they dined on veal and baby corn on the cobs, which Vixen joyfully speared with her fork. Throughout the lunch, as Gewalt explained exactly what measures had already been taken to protect the Russians, his look became gradually more worried, despite the youthful delights of the food spread before him.

'The main problem is that the Russian guests refyuse absolutely to have guards on their own floor,' he said, looking at Fox-Foetus for some support.

'Why is that?' asked the chief superintendent.

'They refyuse to believe that they are under threat of attack,' said Gewalt. 'And in any case it is *so* difficult to make them understand anything I say. Ve have no Russian speakers here, and they do not speak German.'

'This is an unusual problem,' said the chief superintendent. He pondered for a moment, and then, as if to demonstrate the genius of the *protégée* by his side, said, 'What do you recommend, Miss Vixen?'

Vixen looked at her mate and then at his nose. A young waiter came up with some more wine, but tripped and broke the bottle. Gewalt sent him away to be flogged.

'Then we must force our security on them,' said Vixen.

'Yes, I agree, we should indeed consider doing that,' said Gewalt. 'You must realise, you know, the importance of this delegation. They are all here to attend a conference in the Nord-Rhein Vestfalen parliament in town. Bonn sees it as a major breakthrough in East-Vest relations. When the local police were informed of the threat, they immediately send an extra fifty officers to the hotel.'

'But I presume that something special needs to be set in motion in this case,' said Fox-Foetus slowly.

'Indeed,' said Gewalt.

'Let us go and inspect the floor for ourselves,' said the efficient chief superintendent. 'Which one was it, did you say?'

'Floor ten,' said Gewalt. 'Indeed.'

So after lunch the trio took the service lift to the tenth floor, which they had to reach by going through the kitchen.

'I try to avoid the guest lift vhen I visit the Russians,' said Gewalt. 'They never use it themselves, you see, because they think it too bourgeois. So we must ascend with all the ordinary workers.'

Vixen suppressed a complaining groan at this stage, and they went through the kitchen. Fox-Foetus was pleased to note that it was designed in exactly the same way as the one in the London Gloria, even down to the uniforms of the workers. The only difference was that all the vicious calls and oaths were, of course, being administered in German. Otherwise, it might have been possible to believe that they were back once more in the murky, squalid depths of the London hotel.

Like all large hotels all floors of the Düsseldorf Gloria could be reached by both a guest lift (decorated with scrolls and pink wallpaper) and by the service lift (decorated with cigarette ends and small decomposing piles of food). This was the lift used by the chambermaids, the waiters on room service, and the lower staff of the hotel. It was most unusual for people such as the manager to use it, but word had already got round about the Russian's anti-bourgeois tendencies.

'Really, Pickly,' said Vixen, as the old lift rattled on its slow way upwards, 'I think these Russian fellows might have chosen some other place to show their absurd political sentiments. I have a terrible feeling that this lift is going to fall to the ground. It *is* safe, isn't it?' she demanded of Gewalt.

'Oh yes, indeed,' said Gewalt, smiling unpleasantly. 'Most safe.' He did not mention that the lift cable broke, on average, five times a year, killing surplus personnel. 'But indeed, it would not be vise to disobey these Russians. They are very good customers.'

They did not speak again until the old lift had reached its destination and disgorged them all. The Russians were all over the place, occupying as they did every room on the floor. Some of them were playing chess on little tables, blocking up the corridors, while others were gathered around a blackboard, eagerly discussing in loud Russian what appeared to be some crucial political point.

'As long as ve speak in English,' said Gewalt, 'they cannot understand us, or at least I think they can't. Indeed, the same vould be true if ve conducted our conversation in German. I must say, that I find it very difficult to understand vy they came here at all. None of their party understands German or English. But they do pay their bills, and that is vhat matters.'

As they walked amongst the Russians (who took no notice

of them whatsoever) Fox-Foetus's nose was seen to continually oscillate on its axis, probing into corners and crevices that might present security problems. Vixen saw this, and her heart burned with love for his power. If she watched him long enough, she, too, might one day be as efficient as he, she thought.

'You vill see,' said Gewalt, 'that none of the Russians care in the least about the threat of attack. It took me two hours to explain to them vot voz happening, with some assistance from a drunken interpreter from Vuppertal. But it does not interest them at all. Indeed, all they seem capable of doing is playing chess, talking in Russian about politics, or at least that is vot I assume they are talking about, and shouting at each other.'

'Nevertheless,' said Fox-Foetus, with professional solicitude, 'our job is to protect people, whether or not they wish to be protected.'

'Indeed,' said Gewalt.

Vixen stared up at her lover. What a strength of nose!

'So our Russian friends still refuse to accept personal guards?' said Fox-Foetus. He was looking and nasally staring at a copy of the plan of the Düsseldorf Gloria. 'They still refuse to accept them, despite the warning they have received?'

'Indeed,' said Gewalt. 'As I have said, yes.'

'Then listen,' went on the long-nosed expert. 'This is what we are compelled to do.'

He had become increasingly aware that Gewalt was a complete imbecile, and while he continued to ask him questions, Fox-Foetus made sure he only posed ones to which he knew the answer himself anyway.

'We have already positioned guards around the hotel, inside

the hotel, and on every floor except floor ten,' said Fox-Foetus.

'I see,' replied Gewalt.

'Only this,' said Fox-Foetus, ignoring him. 'Only this remains to be done. Take four of your best guards, make sure they are properly armed, and put them in the lifts, two in each.'

'The lifts?' repeated Gewalt stupidly.

'Of course,' said Fox-Foetus, bestowing an all-knowing glance on his pimple-nosed lover. 'If that is so, how can any possible assassin reach them? Once the lifts and the stairs - including the external fire escape steps - are guarded, the Russians are safe, short of someone blowing up the entire hotel.'

'Oh,' said Gewalt. 'I did not think of that.'

'No,' said Fox-Foetus, with another glance at Vixen. He stood up. 'But do not worry. Myself and my assistant here receive our large salaries because of our special abilities.'

Modest man! thought Vixen. So much more he could have said!

Gewalt was still staring at the blueprint plan.

'So if we are to guard the lifts, stairs and the fire escape,' he said, 'there is no other vay the assassins could reach the Russians?'

'No,' said Fox-Foetus, turning contemptuously as he reached the door. 'No other way is possible at all.'

When Vixen and her efficient mentor were heading towards the hotel foyer, there was a loud breathing noise beside them. Fox-Foetus turned round, and saw a very old, shrivelled-looking man, who was making supplicating gestures with long, scaly arms towards the chief superintendent. Fox-Foetus looked harder. The old man was well dressed, certainly not another Assistant Menial, but he seemed to be exceedingly exhausted.

'Please. Please,' said the old man. 'Please wait.' He breathed very loud, long panting breaths, and raised a hand again to still the duo's movements.

'Yes?' said the chief superintendent.

'Wait… wait,' repeated the old man. He breathed a little more, and then said, 'Good, good, I have finally met you. I have been all over this accursed city, trying to find where you were.'

'Sir,' said Fox-Foetus. 'My assistant and I have had a tiring day and…'

'Wait,' interrupted the old man, with surprising volume, considering his age. 'Let me make myself known to you. I am Dr Tortoise. I am acquainted with Chief Inspector Geddem. It is I who am responsible for raising this alarm.'

Fox-Foetus stared at Tortoise for some time, then said, 'How did you come by your information? This was something my friend Chief Inspector Geddem did not make sufficiently clear in our telephone conversation.'

'There is a man I have employed, by the name of Terrapin. He is at present pursuing the Finns, and it was from him that I received information about the attack.'

'Is this Terrapin trained in matters of security?'

Tortoise's mind swung back to his memory of the ragged figure who had accepted the Proconsul card, and the mission. Tortoise regarded Terrapin with a certain reverence, and even affection. The old man did not want to cast any slur on Charles's character.

'He is not trained by any recognised body. But he is trained.' Tortoise left doubt hanging in the air.

'I assure you, Dr Tortoise,' Fox-Foetus said, 'that we will at the very least capture these would-be violent terrorists. It is impossible for them to reach their objective without encountering one or more of the guards I have positioned. I will shortly be returning to the hotel, where we will wait for their arrival.'

'If you catch them,' said Tortoise. 'That will be good. But perhaps Terrapin will eliminate them beforehand, or is in the process of doing so.'

'Thank you for telling us of the plot,' said Fox-Foetus, feeling that it was expected of him.

'Me! Don't thank me! I want those Finns dead. I want them out of the world they pollute with their existence. I have good reason to want that, goodness knows.'

The old man wiped his brow, muttering to himself. Finally he shook his head rapidly a few times, as if jerking himself back to some sort of life.

Tortoise stood up. 'I am staying here in Room 1313,' he said.

'Thank you, Dr Tortoise,' said Fox-Foetus, in an unusually
She shook hands with Tortoise, Fox-Foetus could not help but notice, with what seemed like curious enthusiasm, considering how little they knew the old man.

After Tortoise left, Fox-Foetus ordered his nasally complementary assistant a coffee and the German delicacy *Erdbeertorte mit Schlagsahne* - strawberry flan with whipped cream. This came shortly, Vixen having been strangely silent in the interim. A few moments after starting to stuff herself, she put down her fork and wiped the cream from her chin.

'His neck,' she said, quite loudly. 'His neck! His neck!'

Fox-Foetus gave Vixen an astonished look, then said: 'Miss Vixen, may I remind you where you are. It is specifically indicated in the training manual that security officers must remain inconspicuous at all times.'

Vixen shot him an abrupt, contemptuous sidelong glance. 'Oh, do be quiet, Nosy.'

Fox-Foetus simply could not believe it. He stared at Vixen. '*What* did you just say?'

'Didn't you hear me?' she demanded, 'I said "do be quiet, Nosy".' Vixen then shook her head, moaning softly, 'His neck, his neck!' and then added: 'What was that man's name?'

The question was addressed, presumably, to Fox-Foetus, but Vixen said it as if it were a question thrown to the winds.

'His name, Miss Vixen, was Tortoise,' Fox-Foetus replied, in an abrupt, short way. He was sure his assistant had never behaved like this towards him before.

'As he said himself at least once,' he snapped.

But Vixen was hardly listening. She merely stared into the distance, a sort of crazed half-smile on her unpleasant face. Then she quickly gobbled down the rest of her strawberry flan, swilled down her coffee, and stood up.

'*Sit down,* Miss Vixen,' said Fox-Foetus, losing his temper.

Miss Vixen did slowly sit down, but as if a voice from the heavens had commanded her, not the chief superintendent. Once in her seat again, she gazed in a dreamy state around the room. Finally, as if by chance, she looked at Fox-Foetus.

The chief superintendent was staring at his assistant with all of his efficient anger. It was a look that would have melted, and had melted, the rebellious spirit of many a washer-up or waiter, or even junior or middle-ranking managers. But it had no effect on Vixen, who simply stared at Fox-Foetus with a gaze that, now, indicated the profoundest contempt rather than the most devoted affection.

'How wrong I was,' she began. 'And all the time, living in the same country as me, there was that wonderful man.'

'Eh?' asked the chief superintendent. For the first time in his thirty-year career he had nothing whatsoever to say. Had someone put something in the strawberry flan? Or maybe it was the stress of their German assignment that was causing his assistant to behave in such a strange manner? Finally, he said, in a rather lower voice than usual:

'Miss Vixen. You seem to be in some distress… I am sure that any problem you have can be rectified later, when we are by ourselves, in our room.'

And then, influenced by the peculiar situation and because he thought that things needed more direct action, Fox-Foetus rubbed the right side of his nose with his right forefinger. It was his deepest gesture on behalf of sexual passion and that mysterious loyalty that humans call love.

Vixen drew her head back. She seemed to be seeing him for the first time in their sordid liaison.

'Your nose…' she began.

Fox-Foetus smiled to himself, pleased that his gesture had had the required effect, although he would have preferred Vixen not to have mentioned his much-prized possession by name.

'It's bloody enormous,' said Vixen.

'What?'

'Your nose. It's the longest thing I've ever seen. It's gigantic. It makes the River Rhine look like a puddle. It stretches out from you like a lighthouse that's fallen over.'

By this time Fox-Foetus was convinced his assistant had completely lost her mind. 'Miss VIXEN!' he snapped, in an efficient abrupt hiss.

'Don't you *Miss Vixen* me,' retorted the nymph, loudly. 'Don't you prod your massive nose at me! I won't be prodded. Especially not by such a protuberance as yours.'

'Leave my nose out of this, Miss Vixen. I am at a loss to understand what has happened to you but…'

'Listen, Nosy… Don't you get fresh with me. Just watch what you say, you big-nosed prat.'

Fox-Foetus almost fell out of his seat when he heard this latest appellation. He took Vixen's hand, meaning to pull her out of the café, but she shook him off with surprising strength.

'Get off me!' she bellowed. People around their table started to look. 'Your hands are just about as ugly as your nose.' She glanced sideways at the said orifice, as if inspecting it. 'It's so long!' she exclaimed. 'Is that how you get hold of criminals? Probe them with your nose? Must take a lot of cleaning. Does it?'

'Be quiet!' yelled the chief superintendent.

'OK, Nosy.'

'And don't call me that.'

'Why not? Isn't it the best name for you? It really is *monstrous*. Must be dangerous kissing you, with a nose like that.'

This reference, this denial of their mutual nasal passion, was more than Fox-Foetus's stunned nerves could take. He stood up, this time locking Vixen in a half-Nelson that she really could not break. 'Leave off, you big-nosed fool,' cried Vixen. 'What a nose! You ought to pay more tax for all the extra air you breathe!'

The pair struggled in this way for a few moments, when the assistant hotel manager, Herr Donner, came up to them and told them they were making too much noise and would have to leave.

'It's not *my* fault,' called out Vixen, still kicking, despite Fox-Foetus's iron hold on her. '*I've* got quite a small nose. But look at his! Have you ever seen anything like it?' she demanded of Donner, who made no reply. 'Get off!' cried Vixen, once more, as the baffled, humiliated, long-nosed chief superintendent carried her, spitting and struggling, outside.

Miss Vixen's change of feeling may well be considered to be due to stress, or perhaps to susceptibility to strawberry flan. However, it was in fact due to more romantic reasons. At first sight of Dr Tortoise, she had fallen deeply and passionately in love with his neck, particularly with the tough, brown, scaly skin at the back. With this sentiment overriding all the others in her perverse mind, it was natural that her experiences with the chief superintendent would revolt her and make her display a certain natural antagonism towards the chief object in all these experiences. Fox-Foetus, mainly by bestowing a few ungallant punches in her midriff, succeeded in calming Vixen down enough to get them both back to their room at the Düsseldorf Gloria.

22

The Nose on Legs

'Miss Vixen,' said Fox-Foetus, when that changeable lady was sitting, threatening and fuming, on the bed. 'I do not know what has happened to you, but I would remind you that we came here engaged on a security operation, and the success of this operation is somewhat dependent on you.'

'On me? You really think so? Why don't you admit it, you long-nosed hypocrite? The only person you reckon is important is yourself… oh, and your nose.'

'This abuse will not help anything.'

'You don't think so, Nosy? I think it will. I think it'll do a bit of good. Thought I was just a bit of stuff for you to put your nose into, eh? Well, that's all over, Nosy. And from now on I'll say what this partnership does.'

'I would remind you in what state I first found you…'

'Bloody good state, if you ask me. I was all right, before you put your big nose into things. I was doing pretty well on the London Underground. Could have been promoted to the flogger of people who didn't buy tickets, if you and your nose hadn't arrived on the scene.'

'I refuse to listen to this any further, Vixen. This partnership is at an end. I shall book your return flight. A taxi will arrive for you in the foyer very shortly.'

Making a good attempt at salvaging his professional pride from the wreckage of their broken nasal love affair, Fox-Foetus made himself (his whole body, not just his nose) as erect as possible, and announced:

'A man in my position has a use for a partner, if the right one can be found. But he must also know that he may have to continue…' Here he drew a large breath through his nostrils. '…if necessary, alone.'

'Oh, do close your nose, Nosy. You sound even more ridiculous talking like that than you do when you're speaking normally.'

'You are no longer my partner in any sense. Anything you say is therefore of no importance.' Though he didn't feel that.

'Well!' said Vixen, standing up. 'Since I've got to go, I'll leave right now. But not in your rotten taxi. I'll go when *I* want. But I suppose even you deserve to know what's happened to me. I've met someone… someone else.' She clasped her hands together in a state of religious admiration for the unnamed party. 'He's a real man. He's not just *a nose on legs*.'

This last insult was too much to bear. Despite his reserves of nasal restraint and professional calmness, Fox-Foetus aimed a swipe at Vixen that, if it had made contact, would have rendered her diminutive nasal orifice even smaller than it already was. But Vixen dodged the blow. She made for the door.

'See ya, Nosy!' she yelled, and the last thing Fox-Foetus heard of his erstwhile lover and assistant was Vixen muttering, at the top of her voice.

'Oh neck. Oh neck. Oh Tortoise, oh Tortoise…' all down the corridor.

23

One less guest at the wrap party

Tortoise awoke from a deep sleep to a loud knock on the door of room 1313. He was not pleased at being disturbed. For the first time in very many years he had been sleeping soundly at nights, or whenever he chose to seek rest. It was as if the old man, so long a shrunken mourner for his beloved son, had found new power abroad. With the possibility of the imminent capture of his Finnish enemies, with the chance that Charles would murder them first, his grief had already lessened. He lived now to hear good news from the Gloria Hotel. And then, at last, he would be free.

Vixen knocked harder. During her cab ride to the Hilton she had stopped twice|: the first time to buy a new nylon dress, her previous one being covered in sweat, and the second time to purchase a new red lipstick. Rejection was not something she expected.

Tortoise, an old man, opened the door.

'Oh,' he said, as he saw Vixen. If they were bringing him news, why was Chief Superintendent Fox-Foetus not accompanying his assistant?

'May I come in for a moment?' asked Vixen, her lipstick feeling very wet. She could just catch a glimpse of his neck, when the desk light shone on it.

'Certainly, certainly,' said Tortoise. 'Miss Vixen, is it not?'

'And you're Dr Tortoise, I know,' said Vixen.

'Have you information for me?'

I certainly do thought Vixen. But all she said was: 'Do you mind if I sit down? It was very hot, the journey here.'

Tortoise beckoned her to a chair. 'Have there been any developments?' he asked.

'Not to do with security. Nosy... I mean Chief Superintendent Fox-Foetus, wants me to tell you that nothing has changed since we last met and that everything is under control.'

Then why has she come? Tortoise wondered. 'Oh,' he said again.

'If you knew how difficult it was, working for him,' said Vixen. 'I just had to come and see someone who I knew understood me.'

Tortoise was silent. He had no idea what was going on.

'So I came to see you,' said Vixen.

Tortoise sat down and, baffled, started to scratch the back of his old, scaly neck. It was too much for the enamoured Vixen.

'Tortoise!' she cried, falling at his knees and clasping the old man around his spindly thighs, 'I'm hopelessly in love with you, hopelessly in love with you.' In the height of her passion she very nearly said, 'Hopelessly in love with your neck,' but fortunately she checked herself in time.

Tortoise did not move. He had no emotions whatsoever about Vixen and the old man was somewhat at a loss to know what to do. But he was too soaked in his own newly-found sense of peacefulness to be cruel.

'Get up, please,' said the old man. 'Get up, Miss Vixen.'

His pear-shaped, simian, psychotic assailant returned to her seat, looking for another way to attain the object of her heart's desire.

'I am afraid, Miss Vixen, that I am not at present in the correct frame of mind to return your feeling.'

As far as Vixen was concerned, she did not in the least care what the old man's feelings towards her were, so long as she could have a go at his neck. For a moment she contemplated straightforward rape of the neck, but she decided against it. Although she was doubtless stronger than the old man, the surface area of the neck was too small to make unrequited love of it very easy or very satisfying.

'Miss Vixen,' said Tortoise, who spoke mainly from a feeling of gallantry at not wanting to put the onus on the woman. 'I am aware that there is a love in the world which is held sacred. You, no doubt, are one of those who hold it so. But my own feelings have been gravely restricted by a personal disaster, and thus to love is no longer possible for me.'

He breathed slowly and painfully. The air conditioning in the room was not at all damp enough for his comfort.

Since Vixen was not saying anything, Tortoise felt it incumbent on him to continue.

'I envy your feelings. I have learnt, in my long and unfortunate life, that those with the courage to love are rarely unhappy for long. But the disaster about which I spoke has robbed me of that courage for ever. I am sorry.'

The humanity of this speech passed right over the head and pimple-sized nose of Vixen. She was still pondering on launching an attack somehow. She decided to try getting sympathy.

'So you don't love me?' she asked in a self-pitying tone.

'I am sorry,' Tortoise replied. 'But no.'

Since the word *love* meant to Vixen merely the biting or

scratching of some specific, often peculiar, part of the body, Tortoise's reply was, in fact, doubly in order. But as Vixen saw the tantalising glint of the old man's neck she was seized with a desire that was quite uncontrollable. A plan quickly formed in her base brain.

'Dr Tortoise. I have been forward, forgive me. I wished only to express my admiration for the speed with which you told the police of the Finnish plot. Your deed will save so many lives! Please allow me to record my admiration by buying a bottle of champagne and drinking it with you.'

'Champagne,' said the old man, glad that the woman had not dissolved into tears. 'That would be very nice indeed, Miss Vixen.'

He offered to order a bottle from room service, but Vixen said it was on her and that she would go and buy one from the shop downstairs. What she did not tell him was that she had a small bottle of sleeping tablets in her handbag. Crushed and mixed with champagne they would make a most intoxicating drink and the neck would be hers.

Vixen bought the bottle from the hotel bar, then went into a cubicle of a nearby ladies' WC, and mixed a few of the tablets into the fizzy liquid after opening it, then she headed back up to see Tortoise. The lift cable of the staff lift, which she was used to travelling in by now, snapped on the way back up and she was unfortunately crushed to death. Luckily she was the only person in the lift at the time, nor were there any workmen at the bottom of the lift-shaft who might have been hurt.

Tortoise waited for about half an hour for her to return and eventually concluded that she had been too upset to want to see him again. He went back to sleep, though this time his sleep was somewhat more troubled than it had been before the disturbance.

Fox-Foetus also went to bed at about that time. He had completed, as well as he could, an interview with the manager, which had at least reassured the humiliated Chief Security Officer's conscience. Fox-Foetus was confident that everything possible had been done to ensure the safety of the Russian delegation. The hotel was swarming with armed plain-clothed policemen and detectives, and the two lifts now had a day and night guard on the tenth floor. Fox-Foetus ruefully reflected, as he went to his lonely room that night, on the irony of the situation at hand: that in a moment of great triumph as his security arrangements were forestalling international assassins, his personal life should be such a mess. For mess it certainly was. Apart from the frustration he had suffered in not having had Vixen's body waiting for him that evening, the humiliation he had felt in the café had swollen to an enormous size by the time he went to sleep. Fox-Foetus did not have many human qualities, but the ability to suffer humiliation to a vast degree was one of the few he did possess. The humiliation kept him awake that night for hours. To think that his nasal charms, his beloved nose, had been mocked and abused by that... but best not give her a name. It was enough that she was gone.

He lay awake, his hands continuously roving over his perjured organ. It was large, yes, but it wasn't surely, please, it wasn't *enormous.* And didn't it inhale approximately the same amount of air as that any other human being? He fought hard to rationalise Vixen's abuse. To a degree he succeeded, until he thought of the phrase *nose on legs*. *That* was too much. *That* he couldn't bear. The trouble was that the more he tried to put the insult out of mind, the more he realised how horrifically appropriate it was. All his professional confidence, all his pride in his reputation, all his record of successful arrests, all this fled from the demon thought that embraced him. He spent a tortured night, plagued by visions of a *nose on legs* (about six inches high, with little legs, a huge nose and vast nostrils). And he hardly slept a single snore.

It was in this state that he made the final check in the morning of the security arrangements in the Gloria Hotel. Even here, his ability at his job was so great that, but for a most unfortunate coincidence, there would have been no flaw.

Fox-Foetus had completed the survey of the precautions inside the hotel and marked *'SATISFACTORY'* on his report sheet. In fact, things were rather more than satisfactory, with more guards than guests in the hotel and armed guards on every floor. Just before completing the survey, Fox-Foetus remembered that someone had told him of a small underground loading bay, which was used to collect all the dirty washing which the chambermaids had emptied down the chute. He thought he may as well check it.

The loading bay could be reached only from an outside door, and the bay itself lay directly under the hotel. Fox-Foetus went through the door, and climbed down a long oily ramp that the laundry firms' vehicles used. There was another door at the bottom, which concealed the actual bay itself.

As the chief superintendent opened the door, he saw a sign on it. It was a No-Smoking sign, a long cigarette with a red line drawn diagonally across it. Some graffiti artist had added a tiny figure onto the sign. It was a man's figure, but with large arms and feet, and a tiny, squashed up body. The figure was drawn as if it were smoking the cigarette.

The nose on legs!

Fox-Foetus stepped back, and then peered at the sign once more. No doubt about it. It was the nose on legs. And he was still very tired, and very humiliated.

He was going to open the door and go through it but the sign was too much.

In any case, who would go through the laundry bay?

He wrote *'SATISFACTORY'* against the detail he had on his sheet about the bay.

After all, he was Chief Superintendent Pickling Fox-Foetus.

He had never made a mistake.

24

Waiting for death

The bomb was big.

It weighed ten kilos and was in two parts. Two blocks, covered in silver foil. It might have been a couple of chocolate cakes, ready for a party.

Lahti took the two parts and placed them in a rucksack. One at the top, one in the bottom section.

'Good,' was all she said. 'That is good, now.'

She attached a small timing device with thin wire and put that in a small side picket of the rucksack. Then she zipped shut the top, and tied the cover cords over.

Lahti, Taivi and Silja looked at the bag, as it sat, innocent and waiting, on the concrete.

'Excellent,' said Lahti. 'Now we wait for night.'

She checked her watch, and the three Finns moved back inside the tender, Silja going a little slower than her parents.

From the moment when the main alarm of an impending attack had been given, security at the Düsseldorf Gloria was about as tight as it could ever be. Fox-Foetus's efforts had only in truth made a few precautions a little better. Police were everywhere, ringing the hotel inside and out. No one, but no one, could have got through security cordons after things were set in motion.

That hadn't bothered the Finns.

They had all reached the hotel with plenty of time in hand. By the time Fox-Foetus had arrived, the Finns, and the bomb, had been secure in the laundry bay for three days. With the chute only being used once a week, no other vehicles came down to disturb them. And so the tender lay quietly down there, as hectic operations went on above.

The only person who could have possibly detected it was a chief security officer who had been drafted from the Gloria Hotel in London. But other reasons had stopped him.

There was now only the need to wait. Taivi had planned that the final destruction of the delegation would take place forty years to the day after the grenade had been thrown. So, three nights to wait. The Finns spent the time in clearing things up. They threw Terrapin's body down an old drain.

'Three days, Silja, three days,' Taivi lay his hand on her shoulder. 'Three days. And then, think of the fame and honour you will win.'

'Yes,' said Silja, without enthusiasm. She did not want to die.

'It is natural that you are like this,' said Taivi quickly. 'All are sad before times of greatest victory. Have you not heard how Mika Kivilinna wept before storming Helsinki and setting it free? How he sat in tears before the battle began? And then have you heard the tale of his triumph?'

Silja did not answer. She sat and looked in the distance along the dirty grey wall of the bay.

'Will they remember me, Father?' she asked. Her voice was low.

'Naturally, after our return to our homeland we will sing

of how you revenged us all. They will tell stories of you in the forests, your name will be the only one spoken around campfires. How famous you will be, my daughter!'

'But I shall be dead,' said Silja.

'Yes, my daughter, but for a just and glorious cause,' and Taivi placed an arm around her.

It was an action he had done perhaps only about a dozen times in all of her life. His voice dropped low, to the level it had adopted when he had courted Lahti by the pine trees. 'You, my daughter, shall be dead, yes. But you shall never be forgotten. In our homeland you shall always be remembered.'

Silja said nothing. Since Rod had gone no further stirring of life was awakened in her breast. She was prepared to die without enthusiasm, and without protest. For now that the intriguing young man she had met had been removed from her sight, the vague feelings of freedom he had awakened in her were all ashes. Hints of something beyond this death had vanished. She was once again the girl she had been brought up to be.

On the last night before the anniversary was to be celebrated, Silja woke in darkness. They all slept in the tender, the tender's light was switched off. The girl looked around her. Dimly, she thought how, even now, it would be possible to run away, to escape. But what sort of life would she lead away from her parents? It was unimaginable. To waver from this loyalty to them. But something else was working inside her, and it made her start to cry. She sat up in the tender, quietly sobbing.

Her father stirred in his sleep, and then felt that his daughter was no longer in harmony with them.

'Remember,' he said after moving around a little. 'Remember Mika Kivilinna. What he suffered in the final fight.'

Silja carried on crying and could not stop. Her tears trickled down her cheeks, hot against the chill of the night. Taivi took a piece of old cloth and wiped them away.

'Be strong, my daughter,' he said. 'Think of us. Think of your homeland.'

Lahti also was now awake. 'What is happening?' she hissed into the darkness.

'Nothing, nothing, my love, it is only her.'

'Be quiet,' Lahti hissed again. 'Do you want to give me the curse of fear, crying at night?'

'Go back to sleep, my love,' said Taivi, with unaccustomed severity. 'It is nothing. It is a mood and will pass.'

'I hope so!' and Lahti turned over to sleep once more.

Silja went on crying.

'What is it about?' said Taivi softly. 'What is the reason for these tears. Is it fear?'

'No, Father, no,' Silja managed to force out through her sobs. 'I do not think it is fear.'

'What then, child? How can you cry, on a night that precedes such glory?'

Silja sobbed a little more, then sniffed.

'Sometimes I have such odd thoughts, Father. Sometimes I have such odd thoughts, and they will not go away.'

'Try and explain. It may help to tell me of these thoughts.'

There was a long pause. Then Silja continued, in a much quieter voice.

'Sometimes, Father, I think there is something else, some other sort of love in the world. I think that, despite all you have shown me, you have not shown me that sort of love.'

Taivi's voice grew harsh immediately. 'You think that? But who could have shown you this… this love? Who but us could have shown you it, if it exists?'

Another pause. Then Silja said, very slowly. 'I think that other person could have shown me it. The one who was called Coaster.'

'Him. He will not trouble us any more. It is best that you forget about him completely.'

'It is foolish of me to think these things,' said Silja. 'But sometimes I cannot avoid doing it.'

'Listen,' and Taivi's scarred mouth was very near her. 'You know how we have suffered. All of us. Is that the product of your love from other men? That we should suffer all our lives? Is that what your love can do?'

He suddenly snatched the young girl's hand and rubbed it all over his own face.

'Feel that. There is your love. That is what it has done.'

'Don't, Father,' and the girl snatched her hand away from where it had touched the mutilated and deformed skin.

'Then do not talk to me any longer of love. We are still together. That is enough for us. We are fortunate.'

'Yes, Father.' Silja had reverted to the apathetic indifference of her usual mood. The contact with Rod and even with Charles, had been, she now knew, two cases in her life. They would not be repeated.

'I am sorry I argued,' said the girl. 'I will no longer think of such things.'

Taivi now felt for his daughter's forehead and placed his hand on it.

‘Do not fear, and do not cry. You are brave, and your bravery shall never be forgotten.’

Her father went back to sleep. But Silja sat there, in the darkness, for hours, until the morning. She no longer cried. But her thoughts spun endlessly on. They spun to distant happiness, to dreams of possible joys. She could not understand why the image of her first sight of Rod, with his waistcoat, his jeans and his hair-band, was lodged in her mind and would not go away.

That evening, the evening after Vixen’s attempt to seduce tortoise, Taivi lifted the rucksack onto Silja’s neck. The girl’s face was set in a fixed stare as she went to the bottom of the chute.

‘The tenth floor,’ said Taivi. ‘The numbers are indicated inside the chute. Go among the Russians when you reach them. They will all die. There is one hour before…’ but he did not finish.

Silja looked at her watch. It was exactly eight o’clock.

The chute was narrow, but she could rest the rucksack on one side and push upwards with her legs and feet. She did not say farewell, nor even turn back to her parents as she began to climb.

25

Aching to see Silja

Sloz!

Rod sat there in the motel room, tied to the chair by Silja's knots, which despite all his efforts he'd been totally unable to untie, and wearing his by now extremely dirty clothes, which the Finns had evidently put back on him, though he didn't remember them doing that. He thought perhaps they'd drugged him with something.

He supposed it was the morning following the evening when he'd been tied up. He'd wet himself overnight, being unable to go to the WC, and the carpet by the chair was damp.

As Rod sat, his thoughts wandered crazily around Silja, the Mexican bead-seller, and where in Düsseldorf the Gloria Hotel was, there came a very loud knock on the door. It was so sudden that Rod would have fallen out of his seat if there had been no knots.

Who was it? Was it those crazy Finns, come back to finish him off? Was it the bead-seller, who had found him at last?

The knock came again. Just one, and very loud. Rod didn't answer. He had decided that it must be the Finns, and if he said nothing they'd maybe leave him alone. Or perhaps it was the bead-seller.

Another knock, and this time a call. Rod couldn't speak

French, but he could recognise it, and the language wasn't French. It wasn't Finnish, either: Rod knew by now what Finnish sounded like. Which meant, he supposed, that it must be German.

Well, at least I'm in the same country where Silja is, he thought.

He just sat there. There was some more shouting at the door. Rod didn't reply.

They came in. It was one of the motel chambermaids, with a big bald beefy throb who looked like the sort of person who was called in if there was any trouble.

The chambermaid saw Rod, and the big throb began asking him questions in what Rod was also sure was German. The chambermaid opened a couple of windows. Neither she or the bald beefy throb made any effort to untie Rod's knots. Then they noticed the damp patch and they both seemed to Rod to swear in German, which seemed to Rod an excellent language for that particular purpose. Presently, after pacing around the room for a few minutes and making general complaining noises, the maid and the tough-looking throb went out.

Rod wasn't sure whether to be pleased or what. But it would have been cream to have had something to eat and drink. It would have been cream to have had a wash. It would have been cream to have had quite a few other things. Rod fell asleep for a short time.

This time when he awoke there were three people in the room. The maid, the throb and a grey-haired older grund, who wore a jacket and tie. They looked pretty furious, especially the old grund who kept saying things to Rod in German which Rod couldn't understand. Eventually the older grund got the message and started to speak in English.

‘So vot’s been going on here, then?’ the old grund asked, in English this time.

In the first burst of thinking he had done for quite a while, Rod decided to play it dumb. He could have been Finnish, after all.

The grund with the jacket tried a little miscellaneous abuse in English and then in some other unidentified language. After that his linguistic repertoire was exhausted, and he switched back to German. Then the old grund went away.

He came back a few minutes later. He had a large pair of black shears in his hand, and now he cut the ropes that Silja had knotted so skilfully. Once he had and Rod was free, he tried standing up, which he could do but only just, as his legs were so stiff from being tied up.

The grund handed Rob a small piece of paper, then they all went out. Rob looked at the paper.

It was a bill for a night in the motel. Seventy marks. Rod couldn’t understand any other words on the bill except the total amount, but it certainly was German, not French. Rod wondered how far he was from Düsseldorf.

He wasn’t much worried by the bill. If the bill had only been for seven marks he couldn’t have paid it, as his rucksack, with his money in it, and some spare socks and underpants, had been in the back of the Finns’ tender and was gone.

Rod used the WC, then had a bath. How cream that bath did feel! The downside was not having clean socks and underpants to change into, but he would try to sort that out when he got the opportunity.

Once he was dressed, he crept out of the motel room. The motel was spread out a long way on a two-floor wooden building with wooden steps at each end and in the middle down to a car park, and Rod could see that the reception area was fairly distant. Rod saw that there was a small spinney between the motel and the main road. Rod's room was on the first floor. He hurried down the stairs, headed for the spinney and then to the main road. He had no idea which direction he needed to go in to get to Düsseldorf, but he did know he wanted to get away from the motel. He did intend to pay the bill as soon as he could.

But not now. Now, he was aching to see Silja and to stop her grunds doing what they were planning on doing.

It turned out he was only about forty kilometres from Düsseldorf. He had started to hitch-hike in the wrong direction and had to ask the car that gave him his first lift - the Germans fortunately seemed more disposed to hitch-hikers than the French - to drop him by a roundabout so he could go back in the right direction. Fortunately they spoke English or at least understood it.

Rod needed three lifts to get to Düsseldorf, including the one that had taken him in the wrong direction. The driver in the third car kindly took him all the way to the Düsseldorf Gloria Hotel. Rod arrived there in the early afternoon, about two hours after fleeing the motel.

Düsseldorf was subdued under the sun's glare. Rod was surprised to see a massive ring of police around the hotel, but he went right up to the police cordon.

'I want to see your boss,' said Rod.

The West German policeman he spoke to just stared at him.

'Listen, I know I look stupid,' said Rod, 'but I have

information that could save dozens of lives, so you'd better listen to me.'

'You vill come vith me and see the chief superintendent,' said the West German policeman. He gave a faint smile. 'Just don't make any rude comments about his nose, all vight?'

'Don't worry, I won't,' said Rod.

26

Looking for Silja

Viewed as a nasal abnormality, Fox-Foetus presented a remarkable specimen after Vixen's repudiation of him. Considered in any other light, however, it could not be denied that the chief superintendent had deteriorated considerably.

It was not that he missed his former assistant. The feeling of human loss was utterly beyond his emotional capabilities. But he had suffered humiliation, and this was not to be purged by one sleepless night and by one day bereft of the woman who had caused it.

After making the unfortunate discovery of the nose on legs, Fox-Foetus gave orders that he was not to be disturbed unless something really important happened. He retired to his hotel room, poured himself several whiskies in stiff succession, and avoided looking in mirrors.

A framed photograph of the chief superintendent and his assistant visiting the unfortunately (as they saw it) now defunct execution chamber at Pentonville Prison, which he had allowed to be taken in an unguarded moment, lay smashed at the bottom of the waste-paper basket. Fox-Foetus lay on his bed. He read nothing, in case it should bear reference to noses. He did no work, in case it should remind him of his liaison with his assistant. He just lay there. And his thoughts wandered chaotically and insanely around the emotional vacuity of his mind.

Was he, then, a failure after all? Were all his deeds, the arrests, the tearful suspects, the jailed malfactors, the crying wives, the official plaudits, were these all to be thrown away because of this terrible personal indignity?

It could not be, it must not be. And yet, as the chief superintendent lay on his bed and tried to force himself to concentrate on his successes, only one idea flooded his brain.

His nose.

Its length, width, and the humiliation it had caused him. Nothing, not even the taunts he had received when at school on account of the emphatic protrusion, had been as bad as this. To be subjected to such a fluid torrent of abuse from the very one, the only one in fact, who had previously admired the protuberance so much; it was too much.

Fox-Foetus made little moaning noises on the bed, and vowed to himself that, whatever happened, he would not allow the Finnish assassins to succeed. This case, which had started out as a mere ordinary job, had become a fight to save his pride. He would show the world, he would show Vixen (wherever she was; he thought it strange she had not been in touch at all, not even to mock him) that Fox-Foetus could continue… he remembered his own words… 'if necessary, alone.'

But it was no use. The abuse, not his determined plans, came back into his mind. All day, until evening, he lay helplessly and hopelessly and obsessed about this. A man defeated by circumstances, and by Vixen. No longer the great Fox-Foetus, who had scattered the Gloria Westminster Wine Cellar robbers. A mere husk of the nose he had been.

And now this. A West German policeman bursting into his room after the briefest of knocks, at which Fox-Foetus had sat up on the bed and called out 'Come in!' and then '*Herein!*' - the German word, not the English one - in case the knocker was German. Close behind the policeman was a young male evident lunatic in scruffy, dirty clothes, and with long unkempt brown hair.

'You this throb's boss?' blurted out Rod, as soon as he saw the chief superintendent. Rod was so intent on his purpose he hardly even noticed the nose.

'I beg your pardon,' said Fox-Foetus, sitting up in the bed. 'Are you addressing me?'

Rod looked around the room. ''Course, man,' he said. 'Listen, *I've got to talk to you.*'

The German policeman glanced at Fox-Foetus. 'Chief superintendent, I am Officer Schnell. This young man insisted he had important information vich you vood vont to know. If you vont me to arrest him, of course I vill.'

'Sloz, man,' said Rod to Fox-Foetus. 'This cop's wasting time, and we haven't any to waste. Can I talk with you in private?'

Fox-Foetus, against his better judgment, asked the policeman to leave, but, '*bitte,* wait outside please,' the efficient chief superintendent requested.

The German policeman left, and shut the door.

'Listen man,' Rod said to Fox-Foetus at once, his arms gesticulating wildly. 'Have you caught them yet?'

'Please,' said Fox-Foetus. 'I suggest you sit down and stop rushing about. And I would remind you that I am Chief Superintendent Pickling Fox-Foetus, Chief Security Officer for the Gloria Hotel chain, and that I will not be shouted at.'

'Look man, there's no slozing…'

'And do not use slang either. I understand English, but have had no training course in gutter languages.'

'OK,' and Rod forced himself to sit down on the nearest chain. No point getting on the wrong side of this grund with the huge conk.

'Now,' said Fox-Foetus when they were sitting comfortably. 'Whom do you want to know if we've caught?'

'The Finns. Those crazy Finns. Man, they just about snuffed me out.'

'No *slang*,' and the chief superintendent's nose had recovered a very little of its former glory.

'They almost killed me,' said Rod.

'How?'

'There was this dab, a girl, with a gun and her parents. Man, they're nutty, crazy, the lot of them. They're coming here to kill the Russians who are staying here. Do you know about it?'

'Naturally. We received a communication from a gentleman called Terrapin several days ago via Terrapin's employer, who goes by the name of Tortoise.'

'Tortoise?'

'Yes.'

That was the name Terrapin mentioned just before he snuffed out, Rod thought, in about a twentieth of a second. To Fox-Foetus he said:

'Terrapin! You've got some communication from him? *How?*'

'Before I answer that question,' said Fox-Foetus, 'please tell me your own name.'

'Coaster. Rod Coaster. You've got to tell me: how did you

hear anything from Terrapin?'

'He sent Tortoise a letter,' said the chief superintendent, in a tone of the profoundest condescension.

'He sent Tortoise a letter? But that's crazy, man!'

'Why should it be so ridiculous?' Fox-Foetus asked.

'Terrapin's *dead.* I saw him snuff out with my own eyes. He's gone, man.'

'That,' said the chief superintendent, 'I find most difficult to believe. The gentleman called Tortoise, who is at staying in this very hotel, says that the letter proves he is still alive.'

'Well, Terrapin must have an identical twin then. He was shot in the guts with a shotgun. Anyone who thinks Terrapin's alive is nuts, man.'

Fox-Foetus pondered for a moment, and then got off the bed. He moved to the window and looked out. Below, was a ring of policemen that had encircled the hotel like a giant earthworm.

Fox-Foetus abruptly turned back to Rod. 'Who killed him?' demanded the chief superintendent, quickly.

'Man, there's three of them. Two grunds… a mum and dad, I mean, and their daughter. She's called Silja.' Rod slowed down a bit when he mentioned Silja's name, and he pronounced it correctly.

'It was her,' went on Rod. 'It was Silja who shot him Terrapin, but it was self-defence. More or less, anyway.'

'But even if that's true,' said Fox-Foetus, 'why do you think you need to come here? How can you possibly help us? I will tell you, young man, that all security precautions have been taken. Indeed, I am in personal command of them. It is impossible for the assassins to come within half a kilometre of the hotel.' He smiled down his nose. 'When they arrive, they will receive more than they expected, I trust.'

Rod stared at him. 'When they arrive? You mean they've not come yet?'

'Of course not.'

'But they must have done!' Rod stood up once more. 'They left me more than a day ago! They must have got here by now.'

Fox-Foetus sat down on the bed.

'I do not... I do not understand where they can be.' The chief superintendent was rubbing his hands over his chin and then taking them on a circumnavigation of his nose. In his entire career he had never been so agitated. The dreadful feeling that, somewhere, he had made a Mistake, was becoming more insistent. He looked ruefully at his long-haired executioner, a few feet away. Slowly the chief superintendent's voice changed to one of despair.

'I have checked all areas myself... personally. The hotel has a sophisticated modern design. There are no old passages, or other unexplored places of concealment.'

'The *laundry chute*,' said Rod.

'What?'

'The laundry chute. That's what Terrapin said just before he snuffed out. Sloz, man, I wouldn't forget that. He told me to tell Tortoise... that's it... tell Tortoise about the laundry chute. Any idea what he meant?'

A terrible change had come over the chief superintendent. His normally fairly pale face had become a shade of deep purple. He raised his hand to his proud forehead.

'What's wrong, man?' asked Rod.

Until this moment, Rod had been secretly somehow rather impressed by Fox-Foetus. Now Rod looked, and saw only the nose, which was sagging in front of the chief superintendent's eyes.

'The laundry chute,' Fox-Foetus said it like a man under sentence of death. 'Did he say anything else?'

'Terrapin? Nothing, man. Only that I had to tell Tortoise about it.'

The chief superintendent was sitting on the bed, as before. But he was wrestling with the worst anguish he had ever had to face. For the first time in his life he had made an error. The sign on the laundry bay swam through his mind. Of course. And it had all been Vixen's fault. Her terrible insults had distracted him.

Fox-Foetus called for the German policeman.

'Officer Schnell,' said the chief superintendent slowly, once the policeman was in the room. He sounded as if his voice was being replayed on a tape recorder at a slower speed. 'Please… order all available forces to the laundry bay.' The chief superintendent was struggling with some great torment inside him, but he managed to get it out. 'Immediately… please.'

'*Jawohl*, of course,' said Schnell, and moment later he was gone to execute the command. Now, with the weariness of an aeon inside him, Fox-Foetus picked up the telephone. Rod watched, fascinated. But even as Fox-Foetus was talking, the thought of Silja came into Rod's mind and he had forgotten everything but her.

'Operator… you speak English? Good. Then give me Dr Tortoise, please. He is staying here.' The call went straight through. 'Dr Tortoise… Fox-Foetus here. Dr Tortoise, please listen. There have been developments. Please come as soon as possible. We may need you as interpreter… Yes, I have news of Terrapin. No, he is not here… He is apparently dead… Yes, I am sorry also… Good, then we will see you soon.'

Fox-Foetus replaced the receiver. Rod thought that the chief superintendent had aged ten years since he had first seen him. An intense silence fell in the room.

Then there was the sound of running feet in the corridor, and of shouts and orders in German. A hurried knock on the door, and Officer Schnell was back.

'We have found them, sir. They vere hiding like dogs in the back of the van, down in the laundry bay.'

Rod moved forward. So he was going to see Silja! Sloz! How much he wanted to see her now. Fox-Foetus only looked wearily at the officer.

Schnell turned round, and there was another commotion. Then the Finns, the blighted, cursed Finns, were pushed forward.

Lahti and Taivi. They were handcuffed.

Silja was not there.

27

Redemption

Fox-Foetus looked as if he were going to faint. Rod, who had grown used to their faces, only just managed to restrain himself in time from putting an arm around Fox-Foetus's shoulder.

'Yes, their faces are not pleasant,' commented Schnell.

Fox-Foetus slowly recovered his demeanour. The faces of Lahti and Taivi were frozen into immobile stares. The chief superintendent said nothing. He had finally lost control of the situation around him. There was a silence in the little hotel room, which might have been comical. Only no-one was laughing. Then Rod spoke up, and immediately everyone knew who was now in charge.

'OK, you slozing bastards,' Rod said. 'What have you done with Silja?'

There was no answer. The two immobile horrible faces merely stared.

Rod marched up to Taivi and took the old man by the throat. 'You old splicer!' he cried out. 'Don't kid us you can't speak English. You know enough to tell us what you've done with her!'

He pressed on Taivi's throat so hard, so full of anger at what they had done to him, what they had done to Silja, that a few seconds more and the old man's windpipe would probably have been snapped open. But Lahti had sprung up. Why should she deny them the information? It was too late now, anyway.

'Floor ten,' said Lahti. 'She… floor ten.' Lahti gazed, with a curiously impassive expression, at Fox-Foetus's clock on the table. It was just before nine o'clock. 'Too late,' said Lahti, and she smiled now. 'You… too late.'

'You bastards!' yelled Rod. He pushed the Finns out of the way. Schnell, baffled by so much activity, also moved to the side of the corridor.

'Wait!' and there was a voice from behind. It was Fox-Foetus. 'Wait. I am coming. I insist that I come as well.'

'Then move, man!' Rod shouted. 'She's on the tenth floor!' Rod himself started running on his sloz-strong legs. Fox-Foetus ran too, on thin, trousered legs. Every step for him was a blow against Humiliation.

They were on the tenth floor, up the stairs, in about thirty seconds. Security officers, and even Russians, made way for them.

'The laundry chute!' called Rod.

'Where is it? Do you know?' cried Fox-Foetus.

'You're the throb in charge, man!'

Fox-Foetus instantly pinioned a heavily armed but surprised security officer against a wall and was repeating, 'Where, where is the laundry chute?' like a maniac. The security officer, who obviously understood English, indicated a way through a door. Rod and the chief superintendent ran to it.

They were through. Into a small passageway, with a few bundles of wrapped laundry on the floor. A large hatch in front of them, with a handle. Rod ripped the hatch open. The chute was thin, but certainly wide enough for a human to climb inside. Rod jerked his head forward and down the chute. He could see nothing but the long straight curve of the metal walls.

'Have you… have you found the girl?' said Fox-Foetus, in between fighting to get his breath back. At the door were more German officers. Their guns were drawn.

'No,' yelled Rod, down the chute. He was fighting mad, now. Sloz, sloz, sloz, this was better than splicing. Oh, oh, oh, this was better. Even if anything might happen.

Then Rod heard sobs. Not from the chute. They were coming from a cupboard to the left. A large cupboard. Big enough to fit a not-too-fat person inside.

Another second and the doors were open. And there was Silja by herself. She saw Rod and she froze.

'You're alive,' said Rod. There was nothing else to say.

Silja was silent. Then Rod saw she was looking at her watch. Oh, she wasn't making a big thing of it. She was just peering down at the thin little watch on her glorious wrist.

'Well?' said Rod, almost laughing. 'What's happening?'

Fox-Foetus had stepped up to Rod's side. There seemed to Rod to be a very long pause before Fox-Foetus slowly said:

'I think there is a bomb in this passageway.' Utterly cold and certain.

For a moment, for a few moments, he had recovered his efficiency, his fame, his reputation. He had guessed before Rod why Silja was just standing there, peacefully looking at her watch, despite all the people who were around her. The word jerked Rod back to mania.

'A bomb? A bloody bomb?'

But he couldn't shake Silja, he couldn't hurt her. He just

couldn't do it.

Fox-Foetus was scrambling amongst the laundry. He overturned one pile and then another pile of what seemed to be pillowcases. He kicked a blue bag of shirts out of the way.

And saw a rucksack. The rucksack was flat on the floor, all buttoned and zipped up. It looked nice and ordinary, as if it had just been left there by someone who was going to pick it up later.

Only now did Silja speak. 'I am sorry,' she said to Rod. 'It is timed to explode in thirty seconds.'

Silja closed her eyes, and Rod saw yet again how utterly beautiful she was. And Rod knew that he loved her. Fair and square.

But he didn't touch her.

Rod glanced round to where the rucksack lay. But of all the others who were there, including Rod, only Fox-Foetus was moving.

He knew what he was doing and what he was going to do, what he *had* to do.

Rod began to move now, but Fox-Foetus was already by the rucksack.

The chief superintendent picked the rucksack up. He thought it felt much heavier than it should if only clothes and stuff were in it. So, it was going to explode. Yes, this was it. This really was it. It all came back. All the years of struggle to get where he was. All the work he had put in, all the ability he had shown, all the efficiency he had cultivated. Yes, he had a big nose, but nothing could take away from him the truth: he knew he was very good indeed at his job, and he was right. So, now, here he was with his ultimate test. With his fate, his destiny, in his hands. So, this bomb was going to explode any second now. NOW. So, do something, FAST.

A window, a large glass window, was three yards away. Roughly. Try throwing the rucksack at it, hoping it would go through? But if it didn't, if it bounced back? Glass didn't break that easily.

Yes, so here he was with his test, the biggest of all, the most mighty one he would ever have. And all the others there, all the non-efficient ones, all the Ordinary ones, even this surprisingly focused, decent and helpful long-haired young fellow who obviously had a lot about him and would go far, were standing around, waiting.

Fox-Foetus knew what to do. So suddenly, he knew.

Two steps and he was by the window. Another, and there was glass spilling and tinkling everywhere, as the rucksack went through.

Fox-Foetus was still holding it.

Human bodies broke glass for certain. Rucksacks didn't. Not necessarily.

Fox-Foetus disappeared. Rod, Silja, the security guards, they all crouched down.

Wait.

The biggest explosion Rod had ever heard. Or any of them had ever heard.

So, bang.

And no more humiliation, Nosy. No more worries about being the Best. Because this way you're going out, this way, there'll be no more doubts. No more doubts at all. Ever.

28

Aftermath

'It was extremely fortunate that the bomb exploded in mid-air,' said Tortoise. 'The blast was not contained, you understand, and was far less damaging than it would have been had it detonated on the floor itself, in fact there have been no other casualties.'

Tortoise, Rod and Silja were gathered in the Presidential Suite of the Gloria. They were sitting by a small tea-table, on which were the remnants of a late supper of a spit-roasted chicken, chips and *sauerkraut*, which Rod had never eaten before but really liked.

All press and TV had been vigorously forced away by the many security officers at the Gloria who had been glad at last to find something to do. The Russians had been made aware of how close they had come to extinction, but they had not been very interested. The main problem was that the interpreter had been rather incompetent, and had got so many of the words mixed up. A considerable number of the Russians had gone away wondering why anyone should want to commit suicide at such a pleasant hotel, and with such a very big bomb.

'Was anything left of the poor grund at all?' Rod asked.

'Apparently nothing,' said Tortoise, who had adjusted to Rod's slang remarkably quickly. 'At least, full examination of the explosion debris will have to wait until morning, but at present only one definite trace of the chief superintendent has been discovered.'

'What's that, man?' Rod asked.

'A nose,' said Tortoise. 'A rather long, in fact quite impressive, but of course badly singed, nose. That it should have been found is itself rather remarkable. But I have things still to relate which I think you will find even more interesting. That is,' and a very small smile crept across the old man's face, 'if you believe them.'

By the time Rod and Silja had returned to the ground floor, where they both had met Dr Tortoise for the first time, news had got through that Lahti and Taivi were dead. They had kept cyanide capsules within pockets of skin in their scarred cheeks, and had swallowed them before anyone else had realised what was happening. Tortoise had taken both Rod and Silja under his wing, and had used his money and influence in Düsseldorf to make sure they both received the best treatment everywhere. It had not been possible to get Rod new clothes that evening, but Tortoise promised him jeans, a camel-skin waistcoat and a new hairband the next morning.

Silja was not doing any crying. She had not, so far, said much about the incident. Only, to Rod, that she had felt sorry about him all the way up the chute. And that, by the time she reached the top she knew how much she hated how her parents were willing to let her die.

'As you know,' went on Tortoise, 'I speak Finnish sufficiently well to hold a conversation in the language about most things except highly technical matters. Before they died, an event which, I am afraid to say, I welcomed, I spoke with them.'

He drew a series of breaths that must have been, thought Rod, very bad on his lungs.

'They explained to me how they accidentally killed my son. They explained it all in very calm language. Apparently my boy was having an argument with the father about policies in Communist Russia. The argument developed into a scuffle, and the scuffle into a fight. My boy was, I am afraid to say, rather excitable at times. The mother grabbed my son by the shoulder to protect her husband, and my son fell awkwardly. I believe what they tell me: their words carried enormous clarity. They told me they were terrified about what had happened, and they threw my boy into the sea under cover of darkness. When I questioned them about my son's disappearance, soon afterwards, they were too afraid of my anger to tell the truth. I have mourned my son so long that it was difficult to grieve any more over this fresh information. Now that they are dead, I wish to forgive you, my girl.'

The old man reached out a long, withered flipper-like arm and briefly stroked Silja's face, then he put his arm down and said: 'I also forgive you for your disposal of my employee Charles Terrapin. Yes, Rodney has told me about that. I gather Rodney also told the heroic chief superintendent about what Silja did. I presume, and indeed hope, that Chief Superintendent Fox-Foetus did not have the opportunity to tell anyone else.' He gave a shrug, and a frail smile. 'As for Charles, we must consider the matter as having been fair combat. He lost, and frankly, having met his assassin, I have to say that I would much prefer him to have died rather than Silja.' He pronounced the name correctly. 'No-one else need ever hear of what happened. I may trust to your own silence. Rodney?'

'Of course, man,' said Rod.

'And you, my dear,' Tortoise said to Silja. 'I would hate to think of you having his death on your conscience.'

'I'll try not to,' Silja said.

Rod certainly hoped she wouldn't have Terrapin's death on her conscience for long.

'I have finally discovered,' said Tortoise, 'that grief and an exaggerated desire for revenge solve nothing. Since coming to this mostly beautiful German city I have found myself once more interested in life. My personal health has also much improved.'

Tortoise paused, sitting in the chair like some pagan god.

Neither Rod nor Silja felt that they should interrupt Tortoise's flow.

'I have spoken of what they said of my son,' said Tortoise. 'They talked of something else. What they said at this juncture is rather difficult to believe. I myself consider it merely an attempt on their behalf to claim a victory. I certainly attach no credibility to it.'

Tortoise paused again, looking at Rod and Silja opposite him.

'Listen, my friends. They said that the plan to destroy the Russian delegation was only a way of giving you, Silja, their daughter, some glory. They said there was another, even more important reason, for their coming from Marseilles to Düsseldorf.

Rod leaned forward. He had a funny feeling, difficult to explain but *there*, that there had been something else going on all the time.

'They said,' added Tortoise, 'and I am sorry if it sounds

laughable but I merely translate what they told me; they said that on the way to Düsseldorf they released a poison. They gave it the Finnish name, *hämähäkki,* which means "Spider". They said that it was released into the atmosphere, in extremely tiny particles of bread. Apparently, as far as this poison is concerned, such bread particles are the only way of disseminating it into the atmosphere.'

Rod leaned further forward, his hands on the table.

'They said that the poison will spread for several hundred kilometres from the place of scattering. Then they told me that in Marseilles, there is a further poison disseminator on a beach they know. This releases the poison called "Web". Again, I give the English name. They said that, combined, the poisons are deadly. The "Web" poison needs no bread to disseminate it.'

Tortoise laughed a little. 'A good story, do you not think? Of course I…'

'What else did they say?' and Rod was at Tortoise's knees.

Tortoise was rather taken aback. 'Well,' he said. 'If you really wish to know. They said that the "Web" poison will be churned out automatically once the sea dissolves a wall of brick that protects the controls. They said that the two poisons will combine within a week all over southern France. They said that many people would be killed.'

Tortoise gave another shrug. 'I think, in the end, they did not even know why they wanted to kill. They just wished to kill for the sake of it. But of course they needed an excuse, so they said that this plan was their final blow at the society that had maimed them. Nonsense, don't you think?'

But Rod had stood up, and was breathing hard above Tortoise's head.

'Sil,' he said. He was calling her that now. 'Is there a beach near your home in Marseilles that you know well?'

'Yes,' said Silja, 'but I do not…'

Rod cut her off, even her.

'Please, Dr Tortoise, take us there,' said Rod. 'It's not a lie. I've seen the gizmo, man. I mean, I've seen the equipment. All of it. Please listen, man, please. Take us to Marseilles.'

29

Marseilles

A beach in Marseilles, wide and long deserted, except for a few solitary seagulls caw cawing high above their heads. The sea running in and sweeping out far into the distance, wavetops bobbed and frothed in bubbling loops. The sound of the waves breaking on the shore. A wide sandy beach. And three figures. An old man, Dr Tortoise, walking along like some frail, small, extinct lizard, his feet dragging. A handsome young couple: one very blonde, a young woman, and with graceful, lifting movements, the other hairier, taller, a young man. Tortoise paid for their trip, and for new clothes for Rod and Silja.

'This was our favourite beach,' and Silja stopped in her walking for a moment to look at the sea. She gazed a long time at the Mediterranean beyond them, green and dark and bold and eternally full of enigma and endless promise. 'We would come here whenever my mother's pains became too great for her to bear. We always came by ourselves, we never had any friends. We came out here, and my father and mother would discuss ways of taking revenge.'

'And you say that they had told you of the final plot, the plot by comparison with which the bomb attack was of no importance?'

'Yes.' Silja still stared at the sea. A light breeze lifted her lovely long blond hair. 'They told me of it. They told me how they had learned about the two gases from another organisation. They told me how the gas would be tested on three people.'

Tortoise turned round and watched Silja at a close distance. Now, his eyes were full of a life that had not appeared in them for a very long time. Now, every part of his body was bristling and alive with activity.

'And you say they said the other machine, the machine that produced the other poison, would be left in one of the caves along here?'

'Yes. But I do not know where exactly.'

They had searched all morning. The beach teemed with caves, some no bigger than tiny gaps in the rocks, others large enough to put a man inside. They had found nothing.

'My parents always said that if the machine was put here, then the sea breezes would blow the gas into the land.' Silja stopped. She sat down. Above, another gull, swooping low and soaring.

'What's wrong?' asked Rod. He had not spoken much. The whole search appeared so absurd, so fantastic, so slozing ridiculous. But he had not spoken because, throughout everything, Silja had not let him touch her. She had never said *no*, but he had known, all the time, that he was not to touch. Which was a novelty.

Silja was staring out to sea. She was thinking. The old man sat down beside her. He had all the time in the world. Only Rod, anxious, impatient and baffled, continued to walk around them, stirring up little patches of sand.

Then at last, Silja spoke. 'Rod and Dr Tortoise,' she said.

'We have come a long way, have we not?'

'You bet,' said Rod.

'It cannot be denied,' said Tortoise.

'Will you come a little further? With me?'

'You bet,' said Rod. Tortoise said nothing.

Silja stood up. She was in charge of things now. Rod walked by her side, about five feet from her, as ever. Oh and sloz she was cream… With more purpose in her walk now, Silja headed back towards the caves. They followed. She was silent until they reached a spot where an old tree lay, dead, in the dry sand. They had passed the spot before, but they had not ventured very near it.

Silja pushed by the side of the tree and through a narrow crack. Rod followed her.

'Coming, man?' Rod called out to Tortoise.

'No, Rodney, I shall stay here,' said Tortoise. 'I am an old man.'

'Not that old,' said Rod. 'You're a great guy. We'll be back in a sec.'

Tortoise waited outside. Watching the sea. Thinking.

Inside the gap opened out into a small cave about twenty feet across, with a ceiling where Rod could just about stand up. Silja went to the other side, where the light was not very good.

'Rod, darling, I must be honest and say I was hoping that Ezekiel would not want to follow us. It is important that what I have to say you listen to, you only.'

Ezekiel, Rod had discovered earlier that day, was Tortoise's Christian name. Silja called him that but Rod only called him Dr Tortoise.

Silja fell silent. To Rod, who still stood in the lighted end of the cave, her voice appeared still to be humming across from the walls of stone.

'OK, dab,' said Rod. 'So, relate.'

'Come over here,' called Silja. It was apparent that she knew the cave well. Rod guessed where she was and aimed there. He found himself standing by her. Suddenly, she took his hand.

Cream.

But only to guide it towards a hole in the rock. Rod felt Silja's soft, rather cold hand. Then he felt a hard metallic object. It was shaped like a cylinder, with perforations all over.

'You have it?' asked Silja. 'You can feel it?'

Silja waited. She had let Rod's hand go by now.

'*There* it is,' she said, and bitterness had taken over her placidity now. '*That* is the thing we have been worrying about.'

She laughed. Which Rod thought was pretty weird.

'Yes, that is my parents' last effort at revenge. *That* is all that is left of their cruel Ideas.' She had pulled Rod over to a corner that was better illuminated, and Rod looked at her all the time now, as she spoke.

'You see, my parents thought I had no mind of my own at all. They had the plan of the poisons very many years ago. Of course, it was impossible. Impossible to carry it out on a large scale. But they told me that it was possible, and my father built this machine in the rock, to show me that they could do it.'

Silja laughed again. 'Do not worry, the machine does not work. I knew, quite a long time ago, that this plan was invented to impress me. Breadcrumbs in the air? Ridiculous! As if it could contaminate so many people!'

'I thought it was a bit slozed up, the plan,' said Rod rather feebly.

'More than a bit slozed up,' replied Silja, who had also become used to Rod's slang by now. 'I suppose you might say that my parents were crazy. Yes, crazy. Isn't that what they said in the newspapers in Düsseldorf?'

'But why did you go with them? Why didn't you escape?'

Silja shook her head.

'You do not understand. There is so much that you do not understand. What could I do? I loved them. Who else could I have gone with? And they were so ugly. My mother had pains. So bad her pains were, some days, she would sit and cry all day, sometimes. And I knew why she was crying, though she thought I didn't. She used to look in the mirror, you see,' and Silja turned her face so that Rod could see it full on.' She used once to be beautiful, like me.'

Silja laid her hand on Rod's hand, only for a moment, then removed it and said: 'So they needed me, and I needed them. And there was nowhere else to go. So I stayed. I did not mind. I could have received glory, like Mika Kivilinna did. But you received my message in time. So I have no glory. It does not matter. Nothing matters, now.'

'Nothing!' Rod called out. 'Dab. You're free. We can go anywhere. You're alive, isn't that enough?'

'There are ways of life,' said Silja, 'which you do not understand.'

'Well, maybe,' said Rod. 'Yes, I've got a lot to learn. But I've also got a long way to go, and so have you. And don't you see? If we can be together, that's all that matters. OK, so your grunds gave you a bloody hard time, and would have been happy for you to have died. But they're dead now. What have you got to worry about? The cops don'r know how Terrapin died, and they'll just imagine your parents did it.'

Silja sighed in a quiet, sad, thoughtful way. Once again in his time with her, Rod thought of the bead-seller's egg.

'Oh, Rod,' she said. 'You are such a wonderfully alive person.'

With no warning, she kissed Rod quickly on the lips. Not much of a kiss. Only a touch. But a kiss.

'I have loved you all the time,' said Silja. 'If you can understand that I loved you even when, under the influence of my parents, I felt forced to say those terrible things to you, then you will begin to understand a little. But some of us there are who are alive. Some of us there are who are dead, even though they breathe. I am one of those who are dead. I hope you do have a long way to go, but I do not. My journey shall end soon.'

'That's just slozing nonsense,' said Rod.

But Silja replied, louder: 'No, it is not.'

'*Yes it is,*' said Rod. They looked hard at each other.

'You think I am wrong?' asked Silja, quietly now.

'I know you're wrong,' said Rod. 'Also, there's something else.'

'Something else? What do you mean?'

'I mean this. *I love you too.*'

Silja went on looking at him for a few moments. Then she said, 'You love me even though I killed Terrapin? You love me even though I would have obeyed my parents' desire that I'd die for their cause?'

'I don't care much about Terrapin and anyway the police know now that he killed that fat guy in Marseilles and also one of the members of VALTA. I'm afraid to say that Terrapin pretty much deserved to die. Anyway,' Rod went on, 'the police don't know about how Terrapin died and I don't see how they can find out. The point is, I love you and I've never really loved anyone before but I love you totally. Are you OK about that?'

Silja smiled more concertedly this time. 'Yes, Rod. Yes, what you say makes me very happy.'

They sat in silence, no more need to talk. Because most of the truths were out, the ones that weren't out were only little disagreements nowadays. They weren't important.

'What are you going to do now?' Silja asked.

'Well, I think we both need a holiday. Tortoise has invited us to Canterbury and said after we've gone there he'll pay our air fares and hotel costs so we can go somewhere abroad where we want to go. He even said he'll give us some spending money when we get there.'

'Tortoise said he would do that?'

'Yes, Sil, he did.'

'Rod, have you noticed that you don't call me "dab" any more? You call me "Sil", as if I was a real person and not just some random girl.'

Rod went over to her and held her in his arms. 'I really do love you, Sil,' he said quietly. 'You're not just some random girl.'

30

The start of a new beginning

'My friends,' said Tortoise, 'you must begin again. You are in love, which is very good. You are both young. You have all your lives ahead of you. The money I am giving you is enough for you to use to live on for several months without having to worry about working. When you have both decided where you want to live, let me know and I will give you both a deposit for a house or an apartment.'

Silja went over to Tortoise and kissed him on his gnarled forehead. But at least she was focusing on that relatively respectable part of his anatomy, rather than on his neck as Vixen had. 'Oh, you are so wonderful. Thank you so much for all you've done for us.'

'I am very happy to do it, I assure you,' Tortoise replied. 'I am sorry I hated your parents and their friends because I thought they killed my son, although now I know that it was an accident. I regret how vindictive I was. But at least I can claim not to have caused anyone's death, at least directly.'

'Man, you're a really good guy,' Rod said, 'or at least you are now. Let's not worry about Terrapin or anything that happened in the past. That's then and this is now.'

Tortoise gave a nod, then suddenly stood up from behind his desk in his underground room below the cathedral. 'I shall not be coming here again,' he said. 'I intend to give orders that this room be filled up with landfill and abandoned. I intend to go and live elsewhere in Canterbury. I want a comfortable home with a pleasant sunny garden. Oh, and don't worry, I shall ensure that you are kept informed of my new address.'

Tortoise paused for a moment, then bent down and opened a drawer in his desk. He took out a framed photograph that was about six inches tall and maybe four inches wide. He opened the support at the back of the frame so he could stand the photograph on his desk, so that it faced Rod and Silja. 'This is my son,' Tortoise said. 'My son who might have become…' But Tortoise stopped. He raised his right finger in the air. 'But I will no longer think of that. I am no longer prepared to grieve. For this is where I mourned for so long, for so many years, in this room. All night sometimes, I'd look at this photograph in the half-light. I preferred to mourn here, rather than in my ground-floor rooms. Here I was further from the world and the mourning seemed more appropriate.'

Rod and Silja only stared at the photograph. Tortoise went on, his voice becoming louder:

'It accomplished nothing. Nothing at all. Hatred, hatred all my life, what did it achieve? It left me an old man with nothing. It almost killed you two people whom I love now with all my heart and for whom I will do everything.'

'You've not got nothing, dear Ezekiel,' Silja said to him affectionately. 'You've got us.'

Tortoise was silent for some moments.

'Yes,' Tortoise replied, with a smile. 'Yes, I have you both and I am infinitely delighted that I do.'

He was silent a little longer, then added, speaking softly, 'I have learned, in my long and often distressing life, that there are some who are alive and some who are dead and I know now we must always celebrate those who are alive and do all we can to help them.'

'My God,' Rod murmured, with a loving glance at Silja. 'That's pretty much what you told me, only two days ago.'

Silja nodded. 'Yes I did.'

'Then we are all speaking with the same voice,' Tortoise said. 'Rod and Silja, you are unquestionably two of the alive. You must follow your own paths, and I hope you shall follow the paths together. Now tell me, what are your plans?'

Rod was about to speak but he knew Silja well enough now to know that she would prefer to reply to this question first, and so he stayed silent.

'Well, Ezekiel,' Silja said quietly, 'we're going to spend a few days in Canterbury and then, well, I would really like to show Rod my native country. For very obvious reasons, he has really quite negative perceptions about Finland and I would like to give him a reason to change those.'

'Sil, you've already given me one reason just by knowing you,' Rod interrupted, gallantly.

'Thank you, darling, that's very kind of you.'

'How I like to hear young people in love calling each other darling,' Tortoise said. 'It is a real tonic for the ears of an old man.'

Silja glanced at him. 'I'm glad we're making you happy. I do hope that we can all be friends and perhaps when Rod and I have settled somewhere you can visit us.'

'I would like that very much indeed.'

'Also,' Silja went on. 'I want to show Helsinki to Rod and then some of Finland's wonderful countryside and perhaps even Lapland too.'

'I can't wait,' Rod said. 'I've even learnt a bit of Finnish.'

'Yes,' Silja said with a smile. 'He can now say "I love you" in Finnish.'

'Please do so, Rod,' Tortoise said. 'I know the Finnish phrase of course but I have never had occasion to use it.'

Rod smiled, and, speaking carefully and slowly to Silja said, '*Minä rakastan sinua.*'

Silja turned to Rod and smiled at him. 'And I will say the same to you, Rod darling. *Minä rakastan sinua.*'

Tortoise gave a smile and rubbed his hands together in what seemed to Rod an expression of utter happiness.

'I very much hope you both enjoy your time in Canterbury and your stay in Finland,' Tortoise said. 'Please do come to see me again before you leave Canterbury.'

'Of course we will, Dr Tortoise,' Silja said.

'You bet,' added Rod.

'Thank you. Here is a cheque made payable to Rod which will take care of all the financial matters that I have mentioned. Very well, I will see you out and, as I say, I do hope you will visit me again before you leave Canterbury.'

Rod didn't have a pocket in his outfit so he handed the cheque to Silja, who put it in her white leather handbag. He was already learning to let her help him when it came to practical matters. There would have been a time when he might have wondered if he would ever see the cheque again or would ever get cash but not any more: now, they were collaborating. Tortoise showed them out to the front door of his strange home. Rod shook Tortoise's frail right hand and Silja kissed Tortoise's left cheek and murmured, 'thanks for everything, Ezekiel'. Rod and Silja walked, hand in hand, with slow wandering steps, out into the bright afternoon Canterbury sunlight.

They explored Canterbury with great delight: the Cathedral precinct, the shops, the wonderful High Street that leads to St Peter's Street and the medieval bridge over the Stour with its view of what people boating through Canterbury would have seen in the Middle Ages. Later, by the Westgate and the other branch of the Stour, Rod and Silja went punting, or rather a student from the University of Kent punted them along the shallow water and they lay next to each other and felt they were in paradise.

That evening they had supper at the Weavers' restaurant by the slowly flowing Stour with its gently swaying pondweed and darting dace and chub. After that they returned to their room at the County Hotel. Tortoise had paid for three nights for them in the room and for the first time they made love, and it really seemed to Rod like making love, not just another sloz. They didn't even take any precautions; Silja had told him that if she were to get pregnant, she couldn't imagine a better father than Rod and he felt honoured beyond comprehension that she had said that to him.

Rod never used the word 'sloz' ever again, but when he was with Silja and they were speaking of intimate things, he always talked only about making love.

After their three days in Canterbury they flew to Finland. Tortoise's cheque had still not cleared and so the old man used his own Proconsul card to pay for their flights and their first week's stay in a five-star hotel in Helsinki. Rod never thought life could be as wonderful as this, and while he did give some thought to the Mexican bead-seller, he felt that he, Rod, had moved on.

He was utterly enchanted by Helsinki. He had had no idea what the Finnish capital would be like but he discovered it was relatively small and compact, and unutterably beautiful with its long boulevards from their hotel, its splendid old-fashioned architecture, the boulevards that led down to the market square by the sea; the numerous market stalls and the huge liners in the background that went to Sweden and beyond.

One afternoon, during their week in Helsinki, they visited the Kappeli café, where Silja said the great composer Sibelius had often had coffee and cake with his friends.

Silja told Rod about Sibelius's great symphonic poem *Finlandia* and later that afternoon they went into a record shop where Silja said, like in most Finnish record shops, you could listen to music, free of charge, in a private booth. They found a record shop and went in and listened to *Finlandia* together. Rod had never paid any attention to classical music, only to rock, and he was moved beyond utterance by the melody and the prodigious energy and genius of the piece. He was in tears by the time it finished.

Later that evening, in bed together, Silja consoled him. That was the start of their new life together.

THE END

Weston-on-the-Green
Bicester, Oxfordshire
July - September 1979
and Canterbury, Kent, May - September 2019
and June - August 2020

AFTERWORD

As I said earlier, I rewrote the ending of *Rollercoaster* completely, as my original ending struck me, in 2019, as pretty stupid. In that original ending, Silja died for no particular reason (though not from the bomb blast) other than perhaps to appease my own virginal fears about the sexual power and potency of women (which experience has shown me to be potent indeed) and perhaps also due to some weird subconscious desire on my part not to allow my rather crazy but somehow likeable heroine to survive the end of the story.

Nowadays, while my awe of women is undiminished, and indeed greater than it was in 1979, and my virginal fears are no longer intact, I did want Silja to survive the story. I also wanted the book to have a happy ending.

I tend to believe that all stories should have happy endings, even tragic ones where there should be some joyous insights, amidst the tragedy and disaster. Even *King Lear,* for example, for all the death and disaster at the end, doesn't demoralise us because we find the ending deeply uplifting, for we realise that Cordelia's love of her father, and the goodness of Kent and Edgar, are greater, and more enduring, than the villainy and destruction.

We don't, after all, invest time in reading a novel and watching a movie in order to be left with a downer at the end. In any case, by the time I'd edited the book to where Rod and Silja are talking together about everything that had happened, I was much too fond of Silja to want her to die. So I rewrote the ending of the book completely, after the paragraph in Chapter 29 which starts with Silja's words 'I have loved you all the time.'

I'll leave it up to you whether you think Rod and Silja are still together now, forty years later, but I believe they are. Now in their early sixties, and parents and grandparents, they most likely live in a nice house a mile or so from Canterbury city centre; a house they bought in 1987 when their good friend Dr Tortoise passed away and left them a substantial fortune. Rod and Silja also have a summer cottage by a lake in Central Finland. They go to the cottage for a few weeks every summer and usually also once or twice in the winter. Rod speaks very good Finnish now, and their children are bilingual in English and Finnish. Silja is still beautiful, and ever since Rod met her, he's never been interested in any other dab.

When I retrieved *Rollercoaster* from the folder it had languished in for close to four decades, I was expecting it to be unreadable. As I've said, I was pleasantly surprised to find it wasn't.

Some of it is, of course, rather silly and immature and not always believable. But quite a lot of it seems to me surprisingly concise, taut and imaginative, and it often even makes me laugh, especially the scenes featuring Fox-Foetus and Vixen.

I just wish there'd been a lady at the time who'd appreciated me.

But there wasn't. All I had was Silja.

James Essinger August 2020

Glossary of Rod's slang

cream - excellent

dab - a sexually attractive woman

grund - parent or any older person

sloz - 1) a sexual partner, 2) the sexual act 3) an exclamation

scraping the tar - hitch-hiking

snuff out - die or kill

splice - make love

splicer - the male reproductive organ

squeeze - the vagina

throb - a man

what's the bean? - what's up?

yawn the mud - to live on the road